LEARN GERMAN

Nicole Irving

Designed by Russell Punter
Illustrated by Ann Johns

Language consultants : Sandy Walker
& Anke Kornmüller

Series editor : Corinne Stockley
Editorial assistance from Lynn Bresler

Contents

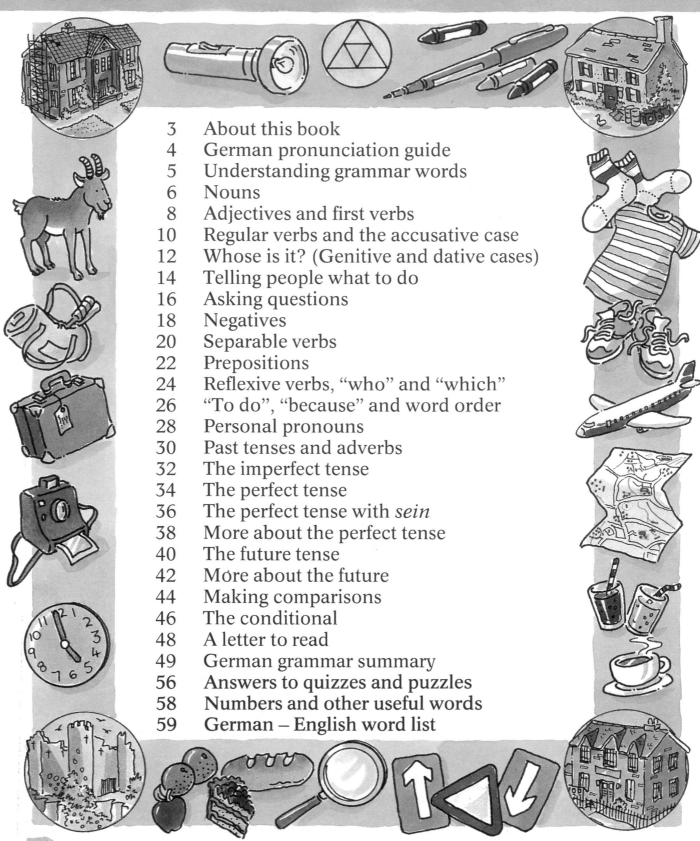

About this book

This book will teach you all the important first steps in the German language and give you plenty of opportunities to practise what you are learning.

Pages 4 and 5 contain a German pronunciation guide and an introduction to grammar. Try out the sounds introduced in the pronunciation guide before you start the main part of the book.

The section on grammar explains basic grammar words. It will help you if you do not know anything about grammar or if you want to remind yourself of what words like "noun" and "subject" mean.

Page 6 is where the main section starts. Each double page explains certain points about German, so your knowledge will build up as you go through the book.

On each double page, the characters in the picture strips say things that show how the language works in practice. The Speech bubble key gives you translations of what they are saying, but you should try to understand them first, and only use the key for checking. Any new German words that crop up are shown in a list with their English translations, and there is always at least one test-yourself quiz to help you try out what you have learned. (The answers are given on pages 56–57.)

In the Speech bubble key, you will sometimes notice a slightly different translation from the word-for-word one. This is because different languages do not always say things in the same way, and the translation given is more natural in English.

The characters

In this book, you will meet various characters. You can see the main ones on this page.

The first two you will meet are Erich and Tanja, as they fly in to Turmstadt from Munich. They are on their way to the Blumenkohl house where they are going to spend a short holiday. Follow their story as you progress through the book.

Erich Müller

Tanja's brother.
Likes walking, climbing, cycling and eating.

Tanja Müller

Erich's sister.
One year older than him.
Likes reading crime novels.

Monika Blumenkohl

Erich and Tanja's friend.
Met them while on holiday last year.

Heidrun Blumenkohl

Monika's mother.
Quite a well-known sculptress.
Runs the house on a shoe-string budget.

Franz Blumenkohl

Monika's father.
Son of Georg Blumenkohl.
Works for a charity.

Stefan Speck

A well-travelled crook.
On file at Berlin headquarters.

Hüpfer

The Blumenkohl dog.
Tireless and brave, if a bit excitable at times.

Kratzer

The Blumenkohl cat.
Inquisitive, likes being pampered.
Loves teasing Hüpfer.

German pronunciation guide

Pronunciation is how words sound. In German, many letters are not said in the same way as in English. German also has groups of letters that are said in a special way.

The list below shows you how letters and groups of letters are said. Letters missing from the list sound the same or nearly the same as in English. Bear in mind, though, that people may also say things differently depending on where they come from.

Learn these tips little by little and try out the words given as examples. If you can get a German speaker to help you, ask them to make the sounds and say the words so that you can copy what you hear.

Vowel sounds

In German, vowel sounds can be long or short. You can normally tell if a vowel is long or short in a particular word. Usually, if it is before a single consonant, it is long, and if it is before two consonants, it is short.[1]

a (short) sounds a bit like the "u" in "fun", for example in *danke*; **a** (long) sounds like the "a" in "father", for example in *Vater*;

e (short) sounds like "e" in "get", for example in *wenn*; **e** (long) sounds close to the "a" in "bathe", for example in *geht*. There is also a third **e** sound which is mostly used when a German word ends in "e" – it sounds like the "a" sound on the end of "Tina" or "banana", for example in *danke*;

i (short) sounds like the "i" in "bit", for example in *ich*; **i** (long) sounds like the "i" in "machine", for example in *Kilo*;

o (short) sounds like the "o" in "not", for example in *Sonne*; **o** (long) sounds like the "aw" sound in "crawl", for example in *Hose*;

u (short) sounds like the "u" in "put", for example in *Mutter*; **u** (long) sounds like the "u" in "rule", for example in *Schule*.

ä, ö, ü

An **umlaut**, or ¨, over "a", "o" or "u", changes the sound. **ä**, **ö** and **ü** can be long or short. The long sounds are explained here. The short sounds are the same, but shorter, or more clipped.

ä (long) sounds like the "a" in "care", for example in *spät*;

ö (long) sounds a bit like the "ea" in "earth", for example in *schön*;

ü (long) sounds a bit like the "u" in "music" (but without the "yuh" sound that English puts before the "u"), for example in *über*. **y** is said like **ü**, for example in *Typ*.

Groups of vowels

ai and **ei** sound like "i" in "mine", for example in *Kai*, *ein*;

äu and **eu** sound like "oy" in "boy", for example in *Fräulein*, *Freund*; **au** sounds like "ow" in "how", for example in *Frau*;

ie sounds like "ee", for example in *die*.[2]

Consonants

b and **d** are usually said as in English. However when they are on the end of a word, **b** sounds more like "p", for example in *Kalb*, and **d** sounds more like "t", for example in *Hand*;

g is usually said like the "g" in "go", for example in *Geld*. However, if **g** comes after "i" on the end of a word, it is said like the "h" in "huge" (just like **ch** – see below), for example in *fertig*;

h is usually said as in English, for example in *holen*. However, when it comes after a vowel, it is not normally sounded but it makes the vowel long, for example in *sehen*;

j sounds like the "y" in "yes", for example in *ja*;

r is a slightly growling "r" sound made at the back of the throat, for example in *rot*;

s sounds like "s" in "sea", for example in *Haus*. However, before a vowel, it sounds like "z" in "zoo", for example in *singen*. **ss** and **ß** are the two ways that German has for writing "ss". They both sound

---

1 Double vowels are especially long, for example in *Paar*, *Meer* and *Boot*. **2** The "ie" on the end of *Familie* is an exception. You say "fa-mee-lee-ya".

the same (like an English "ss"). Between a short vowel and another vowel (long or short), you use **ss**, for example in *müssen*. Elsewhere you use **ß**, for example in *muß* and *größer*;

v is said like an English "f". It sounds like "f" in "fine", for example in *Vater*;

w is said like an English "v". It sounds like "v" in "very", for example in *wenn*;

z sounds like the "ts" in "nuts", for example in *zehn*.

Groups of consonants

ch sounds like the "h" in "huge", for example in *ich*. However, after "a", "o", "u" or "au", it sounds like the "ch" sound in the Scottish word "loch", for example in *lachen*;

chs usually sounds like the "x" in "axe", for example in *wachsen*;

ng sounds like the "ng" in "singer" (not like the "ng" in "finger"), for example in *singen*;

sch sounds like the "sh" in "shoe", for example in *Schule*;

sp and **st** at the start of a word have a "sh" sound before the "p" and the "t", for example in *spielen* or *Stein*;

th sounds like an English "t" (not like an English "th"), for example in *Apotheke*.

Grammar is the set of rules that summarize how a language works. It is easier to learn how German works if you know a few grammar words.

All the words we use when we speak or write can be split up into different types.

A **noun** is a word for a thing, an animal or a person, for example "box", "idea", "invention", "cat", "woman".

A **pronoun** is a word that stands in for a noun, for example, "he", "you", "me", "yours". If you say "The dog stole your hamburger" and then, "He stole yours", you can see how "he" stands in for "dog" and "yours" stands in for "hamburger".

An **adjective** is a word that describes something, usually a noun, for example "pink", as in "a pink shirt".

A **verb** is an action word, for example "make", "run", "think", "eat". Verbs can change depending on who is doing the action, for example "I make", but "he makes", and they have different **tenses** according to when the action takes place, for example "I make" but "I made". The **infinitive** form of the verb is its basic form, for example "to make", "to run" or "to eat". Dictionaries and word lists normally list verbs in their infinitive form.

An **adverb** is a word that gives extra information about an action. Many adverbs describe how a verb's action is done, for example "slowly", as in "She opens the box slowly". Other adverbs say when an action happens, for example "yesterday", or where, for example "here".

Prepositions are link words like "to", "at", "for", "towards" and "near".

Subject or object?

When used in a sentence, a noun or pronoun can have different parts to play. It is the **subject** when it is doing the action, for example "the dog" in "The dog barks" or "he" in "He barks". It is the **direct object** when the action is done to it, for example "the dog" in "He brushes the dog" or "him" in "He brushes him".

There is also an **indirect object**. In "He gives the dog a bone", "the dog" is an indirect object ("a bone" is the direct object). You can normally tell an indirect object because it could have a preposition, such as "to", "at" or "from", in front of it, so in the example above, you could say "He gives a bone to the dog". A pronoun can also be an indirect object, for example "him" in "Give him the bone", which can also be said "Give the bone to him".

To learn German, it helps to understand the difference between the subject and the two kinds of object. This is because German has a system of **cases**. Depending on whether a noun or pronoun is the subject, direct object or indirect object, it goes into a different case. This means it changes a little, for instance by changing its last letter, or the words that go with it change a little. You will learn about the cases as you go through the book.

What is a clause?

A sentence can have many **clauses**. These are different sections, each with its own verb. The **main clause** is the one that could stand alone. For example, in "He shouted at the dog who was barking because he had seen a cat", the main clause is "He shouted at the dog", and there are two other clauses: "who was barking" and "because he had seen a cat".

In German, all nouns are either masculine, feminine or neuter. This is called their gender. The words for "the" and "a" show the gender.

"The" is *der* with masculine nouns, *die* with feminine nouns and *das* with neuter nouns. "A" is *ein* with masculine and neuter nouns, and *eine* with feminine nouns. In German, nouns are always written with a capital first letter.

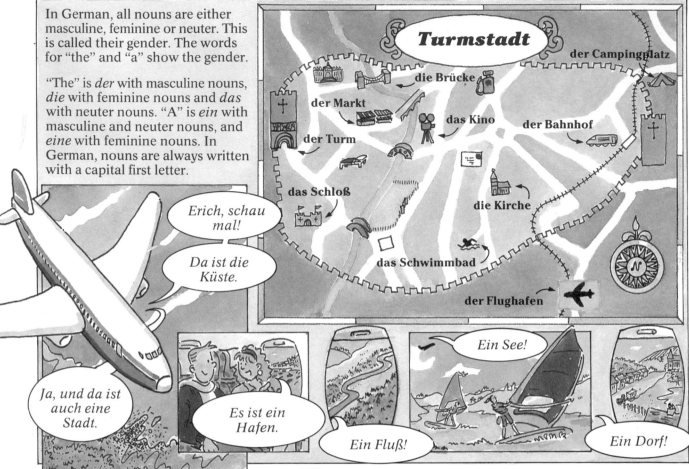

Turmstadt

der Campingplatz
die Brücke
der Markt
das Kino
der Turm
der Bahnhof
das Schloß
die Kirche
das Schwimmbad
der Flughafen

Erich, schau mal!

Da ist die Küste.

Ja, und da ist auch eine Stadt.

Es ist ein Hafen.

Ein Fluß!

Ein See!

Ein Dorf!

Plural nouns

In the plural most German nouns add one or two letters on the end, and some also add an umlaut, for example *die Stadt* (town) becomes *die Städte* (towns).

"The" is *die* in the plural, whatever the gender.

The umlaut

When a noun adds an umlaut in the plural, it is important to remember that the umlaut changes the sound of the "a", "o" or "u" that it goes above (see page 4). The plural umlaut normally goes above the last "a", "o" or "u" in the noun, for example, *der Bahnhof* (station) becomes *die Bahnhöfe* (stations).[1]

Schau! Dort drüben ist Turmstadt.

Berge!

Ja. Da sind die Brücken . . .

und die beiden Türme.

Oh, hier ist der Flughafen.

1 If the noun has the two vowels "a" and "u" one after the other, the umlaut goes over the "a", e.g. *das Haus* (house) becomes *die Häuser* (houses).

Speech bubbles (from comic): "Was ist das, Tanja?" — "Und hier ist das Blumenkohl-Haus." — "Toll! Bonbons." — "Das ist die Karte."

Learning tip

Try and learn nouns with *der*, *die* or *das* in front of them and learn the plural form at the same time. For instance, when you see *der Turm("e)*, learn *der Turm*, *die Türme*. Many words change to match the noun's gender, so getting *der*, *die* and *das* right helps to get other words right.

New words

die Brücke(n)	bridge
der Markt("e)	market
das Kino(s)	cinema
der Turm("e)	tower
das Schloß² (Schlosser)	castle
der Campingplatz("e)	campsite
der Bahnhof("e)	station
die Kirche(n)	church
das Schwimmbad("er)	swimming pool
der Flughafen(¨)	airport
die Küste	coast
die Stadt("e)	town
der Hafen(¨)	port, harbour
der Fluß (Flüsse)	river
der See(n)	lake
das Dorf("er)	village
der Berg(e)	mountain
das Bonbon(s)	**sweet, candy**
die Karte(n), die Landkarte	map
das Haus("er)	house
das Hotel(s)	hotel
das Café(s)	café
die Straße(n)	road
der Weg(e)	path
der Bauernhof("e)	farm
der Wald("er)	forest
die Insel(n)	island
schau, schau mal	look
da	there
ist	is
sind	are
ja	yes
und	and
auch	too, also
es ist	it is, there is
dort drüben, da drüben	there, over there
die beiden	both (of them), the two
hier	here
toll	great
was ist das?	what is that?
das ist	that is, it's

Getting to the Blumenkohl house

For some strange reason, the man in the seat behind Erich and Tanja is looking at their map and memorizing the route to the Blumenkohl house. He's worked out the first of the six landmarks that show the way from the airport. Can you work out the other five? List them in German, making sure you use the right word for "a".

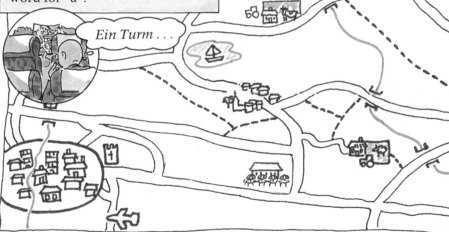

"Ein Turm . . ."

Speech bubble key

- *Erich, schau mal!* Erich, look!
- *Da ist die Küste.* There's the coast.
- *Ja, und da ist auch eine Stadt.* Yes, and there's a town too.
- *Es ist ein Hafen.* It's a port.
- *Ein Fluß!* A river!
- *Ein See!* A lake!
- *Ein Dorf!* A village!
- *Berge!* Mountains!
- *Schau! Dort drüben ist Turmstadt.* Look! There's Turmstadt over there.
- *Ja. Da sind die Brücken . . .* Yes.

There are the bridges . . .
- *und die beiden Türme.* and the two towers.
- *Oh, hier ist der Flughafen.* Oh, here's the airport.
- *Toll! Bonbons.* Great! Sweets.
- *Was ist das, Tanja?* What's that, Tanja?
- *Das ist die Karte.* It's the map.
- *Und hier ist das Blumenkohl-Haus.* And here's the Blumenkohl house.

2 The German letter ß sounds like "ss". For more about ß, see page 4.

Adjectives and first verbs

German adjectives agree with the noun if they come before it. This means they become masculine, feminine, neuter or plural to match the noun. After *der/die/das* (the), they add "e" in the singular and "en" in the plural. After *ein/ eine* (a), they add "er" in the masculine, "e" in the feminine and "es" in the neuter.[1]

Verbs

German has regular verbs that follow patterns (see page 10) and irregular verbs that don't. *Haben* (to have) and *sein* (to be) are irregular. You will use these verbs a lot. You can find their present tense on this page.

Ideale Ferien

ein blauer Himmel

klare Luft

ein klares Meer

ein weißer Strand

TURMSTADT

interessante Ausflüge

Haben (to have)

ich habe	I have (got)
du hast	you have (got)
er/sie/es hat	he/she/it has (got)
wir haben	we have (got)
ihr habt	you have (got)
sie haben	they have (got)
Sie haben	you have (got)

Du, ihr or Sie? Er, sie or es?

As you can see, German has three words for "you". You say *du* to a friend and *ihr* to a group of friends. *Sie* is polite and used for an older person or older people and anyone you don't know well. You always write it with a capital "S".[2] "It" is *er*, *sie* or *es* to match the noun's gender.

Sein (to be)

ich bin	I am
du bist	you are
er/sie/es ist	he/she/it is
wir sind	we are
ihr seid	you are
sie sind	they are
Sie sind	you are

Ich habe eine kleine schwarze Tasche.

He, Erich! Du hast auch ein Zelt.

Ach ja, ich habe ein grünes Zelt.

Oh! Entschuldigung!

Hallo Monika? Hier spricht Tanja.

Ich bin müde . . .

Ein grüner Koffer . . . eine blaue Tasche . . .

Ich habe grünes Gepäck.

Er ist groß.

Wir sind in Turmstadt . . .

Danke, Sie sind sehr nett.

8

1 When adjectives come before a noun without a word like "a" or "the", they add "er" (m), "e" (f), "es" (n) and "e" (pl). In the plural, if a word like "my" is used, they add "en". **See page 50.** 2 In letters, *du* and *ihr* also have a capital first letter.

My, your, his, her . . .

You often use these words instead of "the" or "a". They end in "e" when used with feminine or plural nouns:

(m)/(n)	(f)/(pl)	
mein	meine	my
dein[3]	deine	your (fam)[4]
sein	seine	his/its
ihr	ihre	her/its
unser	unsere	our
euer[3]	eure	your (fam pl)
ihr	ihre	their
Ihr[3]	Ihre	your (pol)[5]

Mein Rucksack ist rot.

Das ist deine Tasche.

Aber nein, das ist seine Tasche.

Hier ist Ihr Koffer, Fräulein.

Mein Gepäck ist grau.

Nein, das geht. Wir haben deine Karte.

What is their luggage like?

Try to find these people in the picture strips and work out what their luggage is like (what kind of bag they have and what colour it is). The first solution is *Sein Gepäck ist grün.*

🗨 Speech bubble key

•*Ich habe eine kleine schwarze Tasche.* I have a small black bag.
•*He, Erich! Du hast auch ein Zelt.* Hey, Erich! You've got a tent as well.
•*Ach ja, ich habe ein grünes Zelt.* Oh yes, I've got a green tent.
•*Oh! Entschuldigung!* Oh! Sorry!
•*Er ist groß.* He's tall.
•*Ich bin müde . . .* I'm tired . . .
•*Ein grüner Koffer . . . eine blaue Tasche . . .* A green suitcase . . . a blue bag . . .
•*Ich habe grünes Gepäck.* I've got green luggage.
•*Hallo Monika? Hier spricht Tanja.* Hello Monika? It's Tanja.

•*Wir sind in Turmstadt . . .* We're in Turmstadt.
•*Danke, Sie sind sehr nett.* Thank you, you're very kind.
•*Nein, das geht. Wir haben deine Karte.* No, it's all right. We've got your map.
•*Mein Rucksack ist rot.* My backpack is red.
•*Das ist deine Tasche.* That's your bag.
•*Aber nein, das ist seine Tasche.* No it's not. It's his bag.
•*Mein Gepäck ist grau.* My luggage is grey.
•*Hier ist Ihr Koffer, Fräulein.* Here's your suitcase, Miss.

New words

die Ferien [pl]	holidays, vacations
der Himmel	sky
die Luft	air
das Meer(e)	sea
der Strand(¨e)	beach
der Ausflug(¨e)	outing, trip
die Tasche(n)	bag, pocket
das Zelt(e)	tent
der Koffer(-)	suitcase
das Gepäck	luggage
der Rucksack (¨e)	rucksack
die Aktentasche(n)	briefcase
ideal	perfect, ideal
blau	blue
klar	clear
weiß	white
interessant	interesting, exciting
klein	short, small
schwarz	black
grün	green
Entschuldigung	excuse me, sorry
groß	tall, big
müde	tired
hallo	hello, hi
hier spricht	it's (here speaks)
in	in
danke	thank you
sehr	very (much), a lot
nett	nice, kind
nein	no
das geht	it's all right
rot	red
aber	but
grau	grey
Fräulein	Miss
gelb	yellow
braun	brown

3 In letters, *dein* and *euer* have a capital first letter. *Ihr* (meaning "your") always has one. **4** "Fam" stands for "the familiar form" (the *du* form). **5** "Pol" stands for "the polite form" (the *Sie* form).

Regular verbs and the accusative case

In the present tense, most German verbs follow the regular pattern shown on the right. To make the present tense, you add a set of endings to the verb's stem. The stem is the verb's infinitive (its basic form, for example *singen*) minus "en" (*sing-*).

Singen (to sing)

ich singe	I sing/am singing[1]
du singst[2]	you sing/are singing
er/sie/es singt[2]	he/she/it sings/is singing
wir singen	we sing/are singing
ihr singt[2]	you sing/are singing
sie singen	they sing/are singing
Sie singen	you sing/are singing

Du gehst zu langsam.

Nein, ich genieße die Landschaft.

Ach ja, die Sonne scheint . . .

. . . und die Vögel singen.

Entschuldigung. Wir suchen Turmstadt.

Das ist leicht! Ihr fahrt hier geradeaus.

Wollen (to want)

This is a very useful verb. It is irregular (it does not follow the pattern above):

ich will	I want
du willst	you want
er/sie/es will	he/she/it wants
wir wollen	we want
ihr wollt	you want
sie wollen	they want
Sie wollen	you want

The accusative case

A noun goes into various cases depending on the job it is doing in the sentence. In German, words that go with nouns may change according to the case. When a noun is a direct object (such as "cola" in "I want a cola"), it is in the accusative case and the only changes are in the masculine singular. *Der* (the) changes to *den*, and *ein* (a) and adjectives add "en".[3]

Ich will einen Tisch im Schatten.

Ich will eine eiskalte Limonade.

"I want to . . ."

You can use *ich will* with another verb to say what you want to do, for example *Ich will einen neuen Pulli kaufen* (I want to buy a new jumper). The extra verb stays in the infinitive and goes to the end of the sentence. *Ich möchte*[4] can be used in the same way.

Er will einen Tee.

Ich möchte[4] *eine Limonade.*

Wir wollen einen Orangensaft und ein Eis, bitte.

Und ich möchte eine Cola, bitte.

Ich möchte zahlen, bitte.

Hast du meinen Fotoapparat?

Was wollt ihr jetzt machen?

Ich will den Markt anschauen.

Oh!

Ich will die Geschäfte sehen.

1 English has two present tenses, e.g. "I walk" or "I am walking". German has only one. **2** Verbs ending in "den" or "ten" (e.g. *finden*) drop the "en", but add "e" before "st" in the *du* form and before "t" in the *er/ihr* forms, e.g. *du findest, er findet*.

> *Wir wollen Fahrräder leihen.*

The mysterious letter

Tanja saw the man drop a letter. This is it. It was written by someone who was really tired and it has lots of mistakes (8 in all). Can you rewrite it correctly and work out its meaning in English?

Eine verlassene Insel, 1893

Mein lieber Sohn Georg,

Ich bin ein alte Mann. Ich bin hier ganz allein, und mein haus in der Nähe von Turmstadt steht leer. Ich habe ein Geheimnis. Ich bin sehr reich. Du bekomms jetzt meine ganze Schatz. Du findst der erste Hinweis in Blumenkohl-Haus. Du suchst die zwei Schiffe.

Leb wohl,
Tobias Blumenkohl

New words

die Landschaft	landscape
die Sonne	sun
der Vogel(¨)	bird
der Tisch(e)	table
die Limonade	lemonade
der Tee	(cup of) tea
der Orangensaft	orange juice
das Eis	ice cream
die Cola	cola
der Pulli(s), der Pullover(-)	jumper
der Fotoapparat(e)	camera
das Geschäft(e)	shop
das Fahrrad(¨er)	bicycle
der Sohn(¨e)	son
der Mann(¨er)	man
das Geheimnis(se)	secret
der Schatz(¨e)	treasure
der Hinweis(e)	clue, tip
das Schiff(e)	ship
gehen	to go, to walk
fahren*	to go, to drive, to ride (a bike)
genießen	to enjoy
scheinen	to shine
suchen	to look for
ich möchte	I would like
kaufen	to buy
zahlen	to pay
machen	to do, to make
anschauen	to go and look (at)
sehen*	to see, to look at
leihen	to hire
stehen	to stand, to be (standing)
bekommen	to receive, to get
finden	to find
zu	too, closed
langsam	slowly
leicht	easy
geradeaus	straight ahead
im Schatten	in the shade
eiskalt	ice-cold
bitte	please
neu	new
jetzt	now
verlassen	deserted, desert
lieb	dear
alt	old
ganz	entire, whole, all
allein	alone
in der Nähe von	near
leer	empty
reich	rich, wealthy
der/die/das erste	the first
zwei	two
leb wohl	farewell

 Speech bubble key

- *Du gehst zu langsam.* You're walking[1] too slowly.
- *Nein, ich genieße die Landschaft.* No, I'm not, I'm enjoying the landscape.
- *Ach ja, die Sonne scheint . . .* Oh yes, the sun's shining . . .
- *. . . und die Vögel singen. . . .* and the birds are singing.
- *Entschuldigung. Wir suchen Turmstadt.* Excuse me. We're looking for Turmstadt.
- *Das ist leicht! Ihr fahrt hier geradeaus.* That's easy! You go straight ahead here.
- *Ich will einen Tisch im Schatten.* I want a table in the shade.
- *Ich will eine eiskalte Limonade.* I want an ice-cold lemonade.
- *Er will einen Tee.* He wants a cup of tea.
- *Wir wollen einen Orangensaft und ein Eis, bitte.* We want an orange juice and an ice cream, please.
- *Ich möchte eine Limonade.* I'd like a lemonade.
- *Und ich möchte eine Cola, bitte.* And I'd like a cola please.
- *Ich möchte zahlen, bitte.* I'd like to pay, please.
- *Hast du meinen Fotoapparat?* Have you got my camera?
- *Was wollt ihr jetzt machen?* What do you want to do now?
- *Ich will den Markt anschauen.* I want to go and look at the market.
- *Ich will die Geschäfte sehen.* I want to look at the shops.
- *Wir wollen Fahrräder leihen.* We want to hire some bicycles.

---

3 *Mein, dein,* etc. (see page 9), like *ein,* add "en" in the accusative masculine singular. **4** *Ich möchte* (I would like) is a polite way to ask for something (see page 46). * Remember, an asterisk (*) means the verb is irregular.

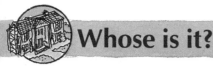

Whose is it?

To say such things as "the dog's basket", German either uses the genitive case or *von* (of, from) with the dative case. The words for the owner (in this example, "the dog") change to show the case (see the cases below). Names are the simplest to use, though, because they never change in the dative, and only add an "s" in the genitive.[1]

Guten Tag. Wir sind Monikas Freunde.

Guten Tag. Ich bin ihre Mutter.

The genitive case

This case shows whose something is. The "owner" noun and words that go with it change into the genitive case. Below on the right, you can see the words for "the" and "a" in the genitive. Masculine and neuter nouns add "s" or "es" and most adjectives add "en". As an example, for "the dog's basket", you say *der Korb des Hundes* (word for word, "the basket the dog's").[2]

Germans often avoid this case, particularly when talking. Instead they use *von* with the dative case and say *der Korb von dem Hund* ("the basket of the dog").

The dative case

This case is always used after a particular group of words like *von* (see page 22) and also whenever a noun is an indirect object, such as "cat" in "I'll give this milk to the cat". In the dative case, most plural nouns add "n" and adjectives add "en". The words for "the" and "a" in the dative are shown below.

Ich heiße Heidrun . . . und hier ist unser Hund, Hüpfer.

Wessen Katze ist das?

Monikas. Sie heißt Kratzer.

"The" and "a" in the genitive and dative cases

	(m)	(f)	(n)	(pl)
genitive[3]	des eines	der einer	des eines	der
dative[3]	dem einem	der einer	dem einem	den

Hier ist das Zimmer meiner Eltern,

. . . mein Zimmer und . . .

das Zimmer vom[4] Untermieter.

Hier ist mein Lieblingszimmer.

Es ist das Atelier meiner Mutter.

Das ist ein Porträt von Monikas Großvater, Georg.

Das ist ein altes Bild des Blumenkohl-Hauses.

Gehören (to belong to)

This verb is another way to say whose something is. Like *von*, it takes the dative case. It is used far more often than English uses "belong to", so when in German you say *Es gehört Tanja*, in English you would normally just say "It's Tanja's".

O nein, es ist Fresser, die Ziege der Nachbarn!

Wem gehören diese Kleider?

Sie gehören meinem Bruder, . . .

12   1 Names ending in "s" or "z" just add an apostrophe. 2 This is the normal word order with the genitive, although with names, the word order is like English, e.g. *Monikas Freunde* (Monika's friends). 3 In the singular, *mein, dein*, etc. take the same

aber dieser rote Pulli . . .

Diese Brille gefällt mir.

Wem gehört dieses Hemd?

Er gehört dem Handwerker.

Sie gehört Tanja.

Erich.

Und dieses Fernglas?

Es gehört auch Erich.

Kleider

die Kleider [pl]	clothes
die Hose(n)	(pair of) trousers
die Jeans [pl]	jeans
das Kleid(er)	dress
der Trainingsanzug(¨e)	tracksuit
die Shorts [pl]	shorts
der Pulli(s), der Pullover(-)	jumper
das Sweatshirt(s)	sweatshirt
das Hemd(en)	shirt
die Jacke(n)	jacket
der Anzug(¨e)	suit
das T-Shirt(s)	T-shirt
der Schuh(e)	shoe
die Trainings-schuhe [pl]	trainers

Saying what you like

German has many ways of saying "I like". The easiest is *ich mag*, from the irregular verb *mögen* (see page 55). Another way is [what you like] + *habe ich* + *gern*, for instance *Katzen habe ich gern* (I like cats), or you can use [what you like] + *gefällt mir* or *gefallen mir*, and say *Dein Hemd gefällt mir* (I like your shirt) or *Seine Shorts gefallen mir* (I like his shorts).

New words

der Freund(e)	friend
die Mutter(¨)	mother
der Vater(¨)	father
die Großmutter(¨)	grandmother
der Großvater(¨)	grandfather
der Urgroßvater(¨)	great-grandfather
der Hund(e)	dog
die Katze(n)	cat
der Korb(¨e)	basket
das Zimmer(-)	room
die Eltern [pl]	parents
der Untermieter(-)	lodger
das Atelier(s)	studio
das Bild(er)	picture
das Porträt(s)	portrait
die Ziege(n)	goat
der Nachbar(n)	neighbour
der Bruder(¨)	brother
die Schwester(n)	sister
der Handwerker(-)	workman
die Brille(n)	(pair of) glasses
das Fernglas(¨er)	(pair of) binoculars
das Werkzeug(e)	tool
heißen	to be called (for saying your name)
wem gehört/ gehören?	who does/do [...] belong to?, whose is/are?
mögen*	to like
guten Tag	hello
wessen?	whose?
Lieblings-	favourite (adds on to front of noun)
dieser, diese, dieses[5]	this, that

Speech bubble key

●*Guten Tag. Wir sind Monikas Freunde.* Hello. We're Monika's friends.
●*Guten Tag. Ich bin ihre Mutter.* Hello. I'm her mother.
●*Ich heiße Heidrun . . . und hier ist unser Hund, Hüpfer.* My name's Heidrun . . . and this is our dog, Hüpfer.
●*Wessen Katze ist das?* Whose cat is that?
●*Monikas. Sie heißt Kratzer.* Monika's. It's called Kratzer.
●*Hier ist das Zimmer meiner Eltern, . . . mein Zimmer und . . . das Zimmer vom Untermieter.* Here's my parents' room, . . . my room and . . . the lodger's room.
●*Hier ist mein Lieblingszimmer.* Here's my favourite room.
●*Es ist das Atelier meiner Mutter.* It's my mother's studio.
●*Das ist ein altes Bild des Blumenkohl-Hauses.* That's an old picture of the Blumenkohl house.

●*Das ist ein Porträt von Monikas Großvater, Georg.* That's a portrait of Monika's grandfather, Georg.
●*O nein, es ist Fresser, die Ziege der Nachbarn!* Oh no, it's Fresser, the neighbours' goat!
●*Wem gehören diese Kleider?* Who do these clothes belong to?
●*Sie gehören meinem Bruder, . . .* They belong to my brother, . . .
●*aber dieser rote Pulli . . .* but this red jumper . . .
●*Er gehört dem Handwerker.* It belongs to the workman.
●*Diese Brille gefällt mir.* I like these glasses.
●*Sie gehört Tanja.* They're Tanja's.
●*Wem gehört dieses Hemd?* Who does this shirt belong to?
●*Erich.* Erich.
●*Und dieses Fernglas?* And these binoculars?
●*Es gehört auch Erich.* They're Erich's as well.

Wem gehört das?

Try to find these things in the picture strips and work out whose they are. (The answer to the first one is *Dieser Trainingsanzug gehört Monika*.)

endings as *ein*. In the plural, they add "er" in the genitive and "en" in the dative. **4** *Vom* is short for *von dem*. You can use either. **5** *Dieser, diese, dieses* change like *der, die, das* in the various cases.

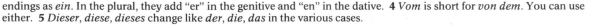

Telling people what to do

To tell someone what to do (for example, "Wait!"), you use the imperative of the verb. There is a *du*, *ihr* and *Sie* form (see page 8). To make these, you take the present tense and, for the *du* form, you usually just drop *du* and the "st" ending. For the *ihr* form, you drop *ihr*, and for the *Sie* form, *Sie* goes after the verb. For example, "Stay here" is *Bleib hier*, *Bleibt hier* or *Bleiben Sie hier*.

Useful imperatives

Here is a list of imperatives that are used very often. Some of them come from irregular verbs, some from separable verbs,[1] and some from reflexive verbs.[2]

du form	*ihr* form	*Sie* form	
wirf	*werft*	*werfen Sie*	throw
sei	*seid*	*seien Sie*	be
paß auf	*paßt auf*	*passen Sie auf*[1]	watch out
mach zu	*macht zu*	*machen Sie zu*[1]	close
nimm	*nehmt*	*nehmen Sie*	take
beeil dich	*beeilt euch*	*beeilen Sie sich*[2]	hurry
fahr	*fahrt*	*fahren Sie*	go, drive

Warte! Langsam, langsam . . .

Wirf das Seil.

Sei brav, Hüpfer.

Paß auf!

Zieht fest!

Machen Sie schnell das Tor zu!

Bleib ruhig, Fresser.

Beeilen Sie sich!

Saying what you must do

Müssen is a useful irregular verb for saying what you must do (have to do). It is used with the infinitive of another verb, and this goes to the end of the sentence, for example *Ich muß hier bleiben* (I must stay here).

Müssen (to have to, must)

ich muß	I must
du mußt	you must
er/sie/es muß	he/she/it must
wir müssen	we must
ihr müßt	you must
sie müssen	they must
Sie müssen	you must

Man (one, you)

You use *man* a lot in German. It means "you" in the general sense of "people", "everyone" or "one", for example, *man muß* means "you must", "people must", "everyone has to".

Ihr müßt alles anschauen – die alte Kirche, die Höhlen, Alterhaven . . .

und ich muß in Alterhaven schnell einkaufen gehen.

Bis später.

Man muß das Tor zumachen.

Geh nach links . . .

und nimm den ersten Weg rechts.

Hüpfer, komm hierher!

1 There is more about separable verbs on page 20. 2 For more about reflexive verbs, see page 24.

Speech bubbles (left column images):
- Das muß das Blumenkohl-Haus sein.
- Ich muß diesen Hinweis schnell finden.
- Zuerst muß ich meine Nagelfeile finden.
- Sei ruhig!
- Diese Schlösser müssen sehr alt sein.
- Sei ruhig, du dreckiger Hund!

New words

das Seil(e)	rope	*kommen*	to come
das Tor(e)	gate		
die Höhle(n)	cave	*ruhig*	calm, quiet
die Nagelfeile(n)	nail file	*brav*	good, well behaved
das Schloß(¨sser)	lock	*fest*	tight, hard
warten	to wait	*schnell*	quick(ly), fast
bleiben	to stay, to keep	*alles*	everything
werfen*	to throw	*bis später*	see you later
aufpassen[1]	to watch out, to pay attention	*hierher*	(towards) here
ziehen	to pull	*zuerst*	first of all, at first
zumachen[1]	to close, to shut	*dreckig*	filthy, horrible
sich beeilen[2]	to hurry	*immer*[3]	always
einkaufen gehen	to go shopping	*richtig*	right, correct

Directions

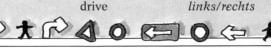

The imperative is very useful for giving and understanding directions. Below is a list of useful direction words:

die Straße(n)	road, street	*gehen*	to go, to walk
der Weg(e)	path, way, lane	*nehmen**	to take
der Platz(¨e)	square		
die Kreuzung(en)	crossroads, junction	*über*	over
		weiter	further
der Fußgänger(-)	pedestrian	*erst-*[4]	first
der Fußgängerüberweg(e)	pedestrian crossing	*zweit-*[4]	second
		dritt-[4]	third
die Ampel(n)	set of traffic lights	*viert-*[4]	fourth
		geradeaus[3]	straight on
fahren*	to go, to travel, to drive	*nach links/rechts*	(to the) left/right
		links/rechts	(on the) left/right

Speech bubble key

- *Warte! Langsam, langsam . . .* Wait! Gently, gently . . . (word for word, "slowly . . .")
- *Bleib ruhig, Fresser.* Keep calm, Fresser.
- *Wirf das Seil.* Throw the rope.
- *Sei brav, Hüpfer.* Be good, Hüpfer.
- *Paß auf!* Watch out!
- *Zieht fest!* Pull hard!
- *Machen Sie schnell das Tor zu!* Shut the gate quickly!
- *Beeilen Sie sich!* Hurry!
- *Ihr müßt alles anschauen – die alte Kirche, die Höhlen, Alterhaven . . .* You must look at everything – the old church, the caves, Alterhaven . . .
- *und ich muß in Alterhaven schnell einkaufen gehen.* and I must quickly go shopping in Alterhaven.
- *Bis später.* See you later.
- *Man muß das Tor zumachen.* You have to shut the gate.
- *Geh nach links . . .* Turn left . . .
- *und nimm den ersten Weg rechts.* and take the first path on the right.
- *Hüpfer, komm hierher!* Hüpfer, come here!
- *Das muß das Blumenkohl-Haus sein.* That must be the Blumenkohl house.
- *Ich muß diesen Hinweis schnell finden.* I have to find this clue fast.
- *Zuerst muß ich meine Nagelfeile finden.* First of all, I must find my nail file.
- *Sei ruhig!* Be quiet!
- *Diese Schlösser müssen sehr alt sein.* These locks must be very old.
- *Sei ruhig, du dreckiger Hund!* Be quiet, you horrible dog!

The way to the old church

Having taken the first path on the right, Monika, Erich and Tanja are here. They need five directions to get to the church. Pretend you're Monika and give Erich and Tanja these directions. The first is *Geht über die Straße.*

(Look at the map on page 7.)

3 To say "carry on straight ahead", you often say *Fahren/Gehen Sie immer geradeaus* (word for word, "Go/Drive always straight ahead"). **4** The hyphen shows that you must add endings to these adjectives (see page 8, and, for the endings in the various cases, see pages 10 and 12).

Asking questions

To ask a question in German, you put the subject ("you" in "you have") after the verb, for example *Hast du meinen Pulli?* (Do you have/Have you got my jumper?).

"Can I?" and "may I?"

Können (to be able to, can) and *dürfen* (to be allowed to, may) are irregular verbs. Like the English "can", *können* is often used to ask if you may do something, although, like "may", *dürfen* is more polite.

Können

ich kann	I can
du kannst	you can
er/sie/es kann	he/she/it can
wir können	we can
ihr könnt	you can
sie können	they can
Sie können	you can

Dürfen

ich darf	I may
du darfst	you may
er/sie/es darf	he/she/it may
wir dürfen	we may
ihr dürft	you may
sie dürfen	they may
Sie dürfen	you may

Question words

wann?	when?
warum?	why?
was?	what?
was für?	what kind/sort of?
welcher?	which?
wer?	who?
wie?	how?
wieviel?	how much?
wieviele?	how many?
wo?	where?, whereabouts?

How to use question words

To make questions with these, you simply place the question word first and then put the subject after the verb as with other questions, for example *Wo wohnen Sie?* (Where do you live?).

Welcher? (which?)

Welcher changes to match the noun that comes after it. You use *welcher* with a masculine noun, *welche* with a feminine one, *welches* with a neuter one and *welche* in the plural.[1]

Modal verbs

German has six irregular verbs that are known as modal verbs. These are often used with another verb in the infinitive which goes to the end of the sentence, for example *Willst du einen Film sehen?* (Do you want to see a film?). You now know the present tense of five of them – *wollen*, *mögen*, *müssen*, *können* and *dürfen*. The sixth is *sollen* (should, to be supposed to – see page 55).

1 In the different cases, these have the same endings as *der, die, das, die*.

Shopping quiz

Try saying all this in German:

I'd like an ice cream.
How much do they cost?
What sort of cake is that?

I'd like a kilo of apples.
Where is the supermarket?
Can you carry my basket? (Use the polite *Sie* form.)

New words

der Apfel (¨)	apple	
das Kilo[2]	kilo	
die Orange(n)	orange	
die Klementine(n)	clementine	
die Erdbeere(n)	strawberry	
der Karton(s)	cardboard box	
der Film(e)	film	
die Apotheke(n)	chemist's shop, pharmacy	
die Bäckerei(en)	baker's shop	
der Krebs(e)	crab	
der Zauberer(-)	magician	
der Kuchen (-)	cake	
die Torte(n)	gateau, cake	
das Brötchen(-)	(bread) roll	
der Brief(e)	letter	
der Witz(e)	joke	

der Supermarkt(¨ e)	supermarket
die Schatzsuche	treasure hunt
probieren	to try, to have a taste
*tragen**	to carry, to wear
wohnen	to live
*sehen**	to see
kosten	to cost
erklären	to explain
mal[3]	(from *einmal* – once)
entschuldigen Sie[4]	excuse me
geschlossen	closed
krank	ill
Klasse!	great!
echt	genuine, real

What does the letter mean?

Resting outside the church, Tanja remembers the letter the man dropped at the café . . .

Monika knows who the writer was, and thinks she knows what and where the first clue is. Thinking about it, Erich and Tanja can work it out too. Can you? Answer these questions and see.

Wer ist Tobias Blumenkohl?
Was sind "die zwei Schiffe"? (Look at the pictures on page 12.)
Welches Zimmer müssen Monika, Erich und Tanja anschauen?

Speech bubble key

- *Guten Tag, Frau Blumenkohl.* Hello, Mrs Blumenkohl.
- *Guten Tag.* Hello.
- *Haben Sie Äpfel?* Have you got any apples?
- *Haben Sie einen Korb?* Have you got a basket?
- *Ich möchte zwei Kilo Orangen.* I'd like two kilos of oranges.
- *Das sind Klementinen.* They're clementines.
- *Magst du Erdbeeren?* Do you like strawberries?
- *Darf ich mal*[3] *probieren?* May I have a taste?
- *Entschuldigen Sie, können Sie diesen Karton tragen?* Excuse me, can you carry this box?
- *Warum ist die Apotheke geschlossen?* Why is the chemist's closed?
- *Frau Salbe ist krank.* Mrs Salbe is ill.
- *Entschuldigen Sie, wo ist die Bäckerei?* Excuse me, where is the baker's?
- *Was ist das?* What's that?
- *Das ist ein Krebs.* It's a crab.
- *Wieviel kosten diese Kuchen?* How much do these cakes cost?
- *Wieviele Brötchen wollen Sie?* How many rolls do you want?
- *Was willst du?* What do you want?
- *Kann ich ein Eis haben?* Can I have an ice cream?
- *Welche Torte willst du?* Which cake do you want?
- *Was suchst du, Tanja?* What are you looking for, Tanja?
- *Wo ist er? Ah.* Where is it? Ah.
- *Monika, kannst du diesen Brief erklären?* Monika, can you explain this letter?
- *Soll das ein Witz sein?* Is it supposed to be a joke?
- *Klasse! Das ist eine echte Schatzsuche!* Great! It's a real treasure hunt!

---

2 *Kilo* is used without a word for "of". It is usually used in the singular. 3 Germans often use words like *mal*, *schon* (already), *bloß* (merely) and *denn* (then) for extra rhythm, even though they sometimes don't mean much. 4 To someone you say *du* to, say *entschuldige*. (There is another, similar word for "sorry" – *Entschuldigung*.)

17

Negatives

In English, you make verbs negative by using "not", for example "I am not tired". You often also need an extra verb like "do" or "can", for example "I do not know" (or "I don't know"), rather than "I know not".

Nicht (not)

The German for "not" is *nicht*. It usually follows the direct object, for example *Ich mag das nicht* (I don't like that). If there is no direct object, *nicht* usually follows the verb, for example *Ich rauche nicht* (I don't smoke) or *Sie ist nicht dumm* (She's not stupid). With two verbs, it goes before the second one, for example *Ich will nicht tanzen* (I don't want to dance).

Darf nicht (must not)

To say "you must not", in the sense of "you're not allowed to", "you may not", you use *dürfen* (see page 16), so, for example, in the *du* form, you say *du darfst nicht*. It is important not to use *müssen* (to have to, must) because *du mußt nicht* means "you don't have to", "you're not obliged to", as in "You don't have to eat the spinach".

Kein (not a, not any, no)

Instead of *nicht ein*, German has a special word, *kein*, to say "not a", "not any" or "no" (as in "no bread"), for example *Das ist kein Hund* (That is not a dog). *Kein* is the negative of *ein*. It has the same endings as *ein* or *mein*, for example *kein Hund* (no dog), *keine Katze* (no cat), *kein Geld* (no money) and *keine Bonbons* (no sweets). This is also true in the various cases, for example *Ich habe keinen Hund* (I have no dog/I haven't got a dog).

Wissen (to know)

This is another irregular verb that is often used, for example *Weißt du?* (Do you know?).

ich weiß	I know
du weißt	you know
er/sie/es weiß	he/she/it knows
wir wissen	we know
ihr wißt	you know
sie wissen	they know
Sie wissen	you know

For "to know" in the sense of knowing people or places, or knowing something like a book, film or song, you use a different verb, *kennen*.

> *Es ist nicht Uli, der Untermieter.*

> *Ach, ich weiß, es muß der Handwerker sein.*

> *Aber der Handwerker hat keinen Anzug.*

> *Wo seid ihr? Das Essen ist fertig!*

> *OK. Wir kommen gleich.*

> *Schaut! Sie sind nicht ganz gleich!*

New words

die Tür(en)	door	*dumm*	stupid, silly
der Einbrecher(-)	burglar	*abgeschlossen*	locked
das Geld	money	*so laut*	so loud(ly)
die Kopfschmerz-tablette(n), die Tablette(n)	aspirin	*niemand*	nobody, no one
		doch	yet, but
		irgendwo	somewhere
das Pflaster(-)	plaster	*guten Abend*	good evening
das Essen	food	*Liebling, Schätzchen*	darling, dear
die Karte(n), die Spielkarte(n)	(playing) card	*allerseits*	(to) all of you, everyone
der Würfel(-)	die (pl: dice)		
die Kerze(n)	candle	*bloß*	merely, only
das Buch(¨er)	book	*hierüber*	over here
der Zylinder(-)	top hat	*nichts*	nothing
		draußen	outside
rauchen	to smoke	*fertig*	ready, finished
tanzen	to dance	*gleich*	right away, (the) same
bellen	to bark		
es gibt	there is/are[1]	*ganz*	quite, exactly
schauen	to look		

Speech bubble key

- *Die Tür ist nicht abgeschlossen.* The door isn't locked.
- *Aber die Fahrräder sind nicht da.* But the bicycles aren't there.
- *Sei ruhig, Hüpfer! Du darfst nicht so laut bellen!* Be quiet, Hüpfer! You mustn't bark so loud!
- *Was suchst du?* What are you looking for?
- *Es ist niemand da.* There's nobody here.
- *Da ist doch irgendwo ein Einbrecher!* But there's a burglar about somewhere!
- *Welche Schiffe? Es gibt hier keine Schiffe.* What ships? There aren't any ships here.
- *Guten Abend, Liebling. Guten Abend, Uli.* Good evening, darling. Good evening, Uli.
- *Guten Abend, Schätzchen... Ach nein! Ich finde keine Kopfschmerztabletten.* Good evening, darling... Oh no! I can't find any aspirins.
- *Und weißt du warum? Die Apotheke ist geschlossen.* And do you know why? The chemist's is closed.
- *Ich habe nichts, keine Tabletten, keine Pflaster...* I haven't got anything, no aspirins, no plasters...
- *Hallo allerseits!* Hi everyone!
- *Ach! Schaut bloß nicht hierüber!* Agh! Don't look over here!
- *Hier sind die zwei Schiffe.* Here are the two ships.
- *Oh, da draußen ist ein Mann.* Oh, there's a man outside.
- *Monika, wer ist dieser Mann?* Monika, who's that man?
- *Das weiß ich nicht.[2]* I don't know.
- *Es ist nicht Uli, der Untermieter.* It's not Uli, the lodger.
- *Ach, ich weiß, es muß der Handwerker sein.* Oh, I know, it must be the workman.
- *Aber der Handwerker hat keinen Anzug.* But the workman doesn't have a suit.
- *Wo seid ihr? Das Essen ist fertig!* Where are you? The meal's ready!
- *OK. Wir kommen gleich.* OK. We're coming right away.
- *Schaut! Sie sind nicht ganz gleich!* Look! They aren't exactly the same!

The first clue

> *Es gibt keine Karten.*

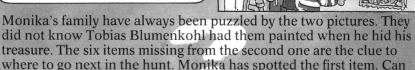

Monika's family have always been puzzled by the two pictures. They did not know Tobias Blumenkohl had them painted when he hid his treasure. The six items missing from the second one are the clue to where to go next in the hunt. Monika has spotted the first item. Can you spot the other five (and make five sentences in the same way)?

Monika knows where to go now. Do you?

---

1 "There is" is usually *es ist* or *da ist* (*es/da sind* in the plural). *Es gibt* also means "there is" or "there are". It is always used with the accusative case. Knowing which to use will come with practice. 2 *Ich weiß es nicht* is also correct, but Germans often prefer to say *Das weiß ich nicht* ("That know I not").

Separable verbs

As well as regular verbs which follow a pattern (see page 10), irregular verbs (see page 8) and modal verbs (see page 16), German also has separable verbs.

Separable verbs

These are verbs which, in the infinitive, are made of a basic verb with an extra word, called a prefix, joined to the front. For example, *zumachen* (to close) is made up of the verb *machen* (to make, to do) and the prefix *zu*. When you use separable verbs, the prefix usually separates off and goes to the end of the sentence, for example *Er macht die Tür zu* (He closes the door). These verbs can be regular or irregular, depending on the basic verb the prefix is attached to.

Common prefixes

To help you spot separable verbs, here is a list of common prefixes:

ab, an, auf, aus, ein, hinein, herein, her, hierher, hin, dahin, dorthin, los, nach, weg, um, herum, zu.[1]

The prefixes can have various meanings. These are best learned gradually. Some prefixes can also be words in their own right (see page 22).

The next day at The Magician Inn . . .

Wann fangen die Prüfungen an?

Dürfen sie dein Eis aufessen?

Sch . . . Ich denke nach.

Fang schon an.

Helgas Zug kommt bald an.

New words

die Prüfung(en)	exam(ination)
der Zug(¨e)	train
der Fußball	football
der Käse	cheese
Pommes frites [pl]	**chips, French fries**
das Gemüse	vegetables
das Kind(er)	child, kid
das Foto(s)	photo
die Schüssel(n)	bowl
die Suppe(n)	soup
der Film(e)	film
anfangen* (fängt an)	to start, to begin
aufessen* (ißt auf)	to eat up, to finish
nachdenken	to think, to ponder
spielen	to play
ankommen	to arrive
geben* (gibt)	to give
trinken	to drink
essen* (ißt)	to eat
stören	to disturb, to get in the way
Fotos machen	to take photos
hereintragen* (trägt herein)	to carry in
reichen	to be enough, to reach, to pass
abhauen	to clear off
sprechen* (spricht)	to speak, to talk
schon	already
bald	soon
doof	stupid, silly
überhaupt	anyhow, at all
nie	never
also	well then, right, so
der/die/das nächste	the next

More about irregular verbs

Some German verbs have regular endings but are irregular in that they change a vowel in the *du* and *er* forms. For example, *du gibst, er gibt* from *geben* (to give), or *du siehst, er sieht* from *sehen* (to see). The change may just be an extra umlaut as with *fahren*: *du fährst, er fährt*, or *tragen*: *du trägst, er trägt*.[2] From now on, the New words lists show such verbs with the *er* form in brackets.

Learning tip

There is no short cut to learning irregular verbs like *geben*. Make sure you learn the *er* form with the infinitive so you know the vowel change. For example, *nehmen (nimmt)* (to take).

Using *gern*

Used with *haben*, *gern* means the same as *mögen* (to like – see page 13). With other verbs, it means you like doing something, for example *Ich spiele gern Fußball* (I like playing football).[3] However, German also tends to use this method (an action verb with *gern*) even when all that is meant is "I like". For example, *Ich trinke gern Tee* (I like drinking tea) is used generally for "I like tea".

1 Be careful: there are also prefixes that never separate from the verb, e.g. *be-, emp-, ent-, er-, ge-, miß-, ver-* and *zer-*. 2 Note that in the imperative, these verbs don't have an umlaut (see chart on page 14). 3 *Gern* means "gladly", so literally, this means "I play gladly football".

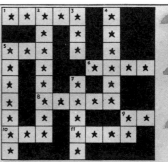

Speech bubble key

- *Wann fangen die Prüfungen an?* When do the exams begin?
- *Dürfen sie dein Eis aufessen?* Can they finish your ice cream?
- *Fang schon an.* Go on, start.[4]
- *Sch . . . Ich denke nach.* Shhh . . . I'm thinking.
- *Helgas Zug kommt bald an.* Helga's train is arriving soon.
- *Sie ißt Käse.* She's having cheese.
- *Ißt du Pommes frites?* Are you having chips?
- *Ja, ja, ich esse gern Pommes frites.* Oh yes, I like chips.
- *Gemüse esse ich nie.* I never eat vegetables.
- *Was machen diese doofen Kinder da? Sie stören sehr.* What are those stupid kids doing? They're really getting in the way.
- *Und überhaupt, warum machen sie Fotos?* And anyhow, why are they taking photos?
- *Paß auf! Er trägt eine große Schüssel Suppe[5] herein!* Watch out! He's bringing in a large bowl of soup!
- *Also, jetzt reicht's! Hau ab!* Right, that's enough now! Clear off!
- *He! Wir gehen.* Hey! We're going.
- *Schaut mal! Ich habe den nächsten Hinweis . . .* Look! I've got the next clue . . .

Crossword puzzle

Each solution is one or more German words. The words you need are shown in English in the brackets. Put them in the correct form for the German sentence and they should slot into the puzzle.

Across

1 and 11. *Sie* (like) *Käse.* (5, 4)
5 across and down. *Ach!* (She talks) *so laut!* (3, 7)
6. (Take) *das!* (4)
8. *Sie* (is wearing) *gelbe Schuhe.* (5)
9. See 10.
10 and 9. *Was machst du hier?* (Clear off)! (3, 2)
11. See 1.

Down

2. (Do you see) *den großen Mann da drüben?* (6, 2)
3. *Nein, danke. Pommes frites esse ich* (never). (3)
4. (There is) *eine sehr alte Kirche in Turmstadt.* (2, 4)
5. See 5 across.
7 and 9. *Der Film* (starts) *bald* (- -). (5, 2)

To do the crossword, trace the outline onto a piece of paper but leave out the stars. They show the squares that you have to fill.

4 Literally, "Start already". 5 Note that German doesn't use "of" to say "a glass/cup/bowl (etc.) of...".

Prepositions

Prepositions are words like "in", "on" or "near". In German, they are always followed by a particular case. Most of them are followed either by the accusative or the dative case. For example, you say *durch den Wald* (through the forest), but *aus dem Wald* (out of the forest), because *durch* always has an accusative after it and *aus* has a dative. The lists below show some common prepositions with the case they need.[1]

Prepositions with the accusative

bis	until, as far as
durch	through
entlang	along, alongside (goes after the noun)
für	for
gegen	against, towards
ohne	without
um	around, at

Prepositions with the dative

aus	out of, from
bei	near, at X's (someone's house)
gegenüber	opposite (can go after the noun)
mit	with
nach	after, to (used with a place name)
seit	since
von	from, of, by
zu	to, to X's (someone's house)

Sometimes two prepositions are used together, for example *bis zu* (up to, all the way to). *Bei dem* is often shortened to *beim*, *von dem* to *vom*, *zu dem* to *zum* and *zu der* to *zur*. Beware: in certain cases German does not use the same preposition as English, for example to say "by train" you say *mit dem Zug*.

Schaut mal! Seht ihr den Mann mit der Glatze?

Beim Ausgang, ... neben der großen Frau in Rot.

Es ist der Mann vom Flughafen!

Es ist der Mann mit dem Brief!

Es ist der Mann aus dem Garten!

Es ist derselbe Mann!

Schnell! Er will unseren Schatz.

Nine special prepositions

These nine special prepositions are sometimes followed by the accusative and sometimes by the dative. If the sentence involves movement to a new place, use the accusative; if there is no movement, use the dative. For example, *Er geht ins Haus* (He's going into the house), but *Er ist im Haus* (He's in the house).

The nine prepositions are:

an	at, on[2]
auf	on,[2] onto, on top of, in (for a language)
hinter	behind
in	in, into
neben	next to, adjacent
über	over, across
unter	under, among
vor	in front of, before
zwischen	between

An dem often shortens to *am*, *in dem* to *im*, *an das* to *ans*, *in das* to *ins* and *auf das* to *aufs*.

Oje! Der Mann mit der Glatze! Da ... vor dem Brunnen.

Er kommt auf den Kai.

Schnell! Kommt hinter dieses Netz.

Ten minutes later ...

Es ist schon gut.

Also, leg den Zettel und die Fotos auf diese Bank.

Hast du eine Lupe?

Ja, aber zu Hause.

Ach, ich weiß! Kommt, wir gehen zu Ralf.

---

22   1 Some prepositions can also be prefixes of separable verbs (see page 20). The prefixes often carry the same meaning. 2 You use *an* (on) for a vertical or sloping surface (a wall, a hillside ...) and *auf* (on) for a horizontal surface (a table, the top of a hill ...).

Ja, ich habe eine Lupe... Sie ist auf meinem Tisch in der Mansarde.

Er ist ein guter Kumpel. Er wohnt gegenüber vom Bahnhof.

New words

die Glatze(n)	bald head/patch
der Ausgang(¨e)	exit
die Frau(en)	woman
der Garten(¨)	garden
der Brunnen(-)	fountain
der Kai(e or s)	quay
das Netz(e)	net
der Zettel(-)	note
die Bank(¨e)	bench
die Lupe(n)	magnifying glass
der Kumpel(-)	mate, good friend
die Schule(n)	school
die Mansarde(n)	attic
das Gebäude(-)	building
die Antwort(en)	answer
die Frage(n)	question

die Kuh(¨e)	cow
der Hügel(-)	hill
der Baum(¨e)	tree
legen	to put (lay down)
wohnen	to live
nachsehen* (sieht nach)	to have a look
derselbe (dieselbe, dasselbe, dieselben)3	the (very) same
oje!	oh dear! oh no!
schon gut	all right, OK
gut	good
zu Hause	at home

Speech bubble key

- *Schaut mal! Seht ihr den Mann mit der Glatze?* Look! Do you see the man with the bald head?
- *Beim Ausgang,... neben der großen Frau in Rot.* Near the exit, ...next to the tall woman in red.
- *Es ist der Mann vom Flughafen!* It's the man from the airport.
- *Es ist der Mann mit dem Brief!* It's the man with the letter!
- *Es ist der Mann aus dem Garten!* It's the man from the garden!
- *Es ist derselbe Mann!* It's the same man!
- *Schnell! Er will unseren Schatz.* Quickly! He wants our treasure.
- *Oje! Der Mann mit der Glatze! Da ... vor dem Brunnen.* Oh no! The bald man! There ... in front of the fountain.
- *Er kommt auf den Kai.* He's coming onto the quay.
- *Schnell! Kommt hinter dieses Netz.* Quick! Come behind this net.
- *Es ist schon gut.* It's OK.
- *Also, leg den Zettel und die Fotos auf diese Bank.* Right, put the note and the photos on this bench.
- *Hast du eine Lupe?* Have you got a magnifying glass?
- *Ja, aber zu Hause.* Yes, but at home.
- *Ach, ich weiß! Kommt, wir gehen zu Ralf.* Oh, I know! Come on, we're going to Ralf's.
- *Er ist ein guter Kumpel. Er wohnt gegenüber vom Bahnhof.* He's a good mate. He lives opposite the station.
- *Ja, ich habe eine Lupe... Sie ist auf meinem Tisch in der Mansarde.* Yes, I've got a magnifying glass ... It's on my table in the attic.

The clue from the inn

Der nächste Hinweis ist in einem Gebäude in Alterhaven. Such die Antworten auf diese Fragen:
Wo steht die Kuh?
Wo steht der Hund?
Wo ist die Bank?
Wo ist der Bauernhof?

When Monika's friend finally finds his magnifying glass, Erich, Tanja and Monika read the note that Erich found in the inn. They have to answer four questions. Luckily the photo Monika took of the painted seat holds the answers. Can you work out the four answers (in German)?

Now can you work out which building they have to go to and finish Tanja's sentence? (The four answers apply to only one building in Alterhaven.)

*Ach, ich weiß! Jetzt gehen wir ********* ...*

---

3 *Derselbe* is really *der* + the adjective *selbe*, so both bits change according to gender and case, e.g. *Wir wohnen in demselben Haus* (We live in the same house).

Reflexive verbs, "who" and "which"

Reflexive verbs are verbs that are used with words like *mich* (myself) or *dich* (yourself), and whose infinitive begins with the word *sich* – see *sich waschen* below. These verbs can be regular or irregular. Some of them seem logical as they are an action you do to yourself (*sich rasieren* – to shave), but many are reflexive for no obvious reason (*sich ärgern* – to be/get annoyed). In either case, English has no real equivalent.[1]

Sich waschen (to have a wash)

ich wasche mich	I have (am having) a wash
du wäschst dich	you have a wash
er/sie/es wäscht sich	he/she/it has a wash
wir waschen uns	we have a wash
ihr wascht euch	you have a wash
sie waschen sich	they have a wash
Sie waschen sich	you have a wash

The imperative is made in the usual way (see page 14) but you keep *dich*, *euch* and *sich*, so you say *Beeil dich*, *Beeilt euch* or *Beeilen Sie sich* (Hurry up).

Warum versteckt ihr euch?

Wir gehen nicht gern in die Schule.

Wieviel Uhr ist es?

Wieviel Uhr ist es?

Es ist acht Uhr, Frau Meyer.

Und jetzt?

Es ist Viertel nach neun.

To answer *Wieviel Uhr ist es?* (What time is it?, What's the time?),[2] you say *Es ist . . .* (It is . . .):

ein/zwei Uhr	one/two (o'clock)[3]
sechs Uhr vormittags	six in the morning
. . . nachmittags/abends	. . . in the afternoon/evening
Mittag/Mitternacht	midday/midnight
fünf (Minuten) vor/nach zwei	five (minutes) to/past two
Viertel vor/nach eins	(a) quarter to/past one
halb sieben	half past six
fünf vor halb sieben	twenty-five past six
fünf nach halb sieben	twenty-five to seven
zwei Uhr zwanzig	twenty past two, two twenty

To answer *Um wieviel Uhr?* (What time? as in "What time's your train?"), put *um* (at) in front of the time, for example *Um elf (Uhr)* (At eleven (o'clock)).[4]

"Who" and "which"

Kurt, um wieviel Uhr wäschst du dich vormittags?

Um halb acht.

Ziehst du dich ganz allein an?

Ja, natürlich.

Ich fühle mich nicht sehr wóhl.

Also, beruhigt euch!

English can use these words as a verb's subject (The boy who/The box which is there . . .) or direct object (The boy who(m)[5] I met . . ., The box which I got . . .). Note that we often say "that" instead, or we just drop the word (The boy I met).

German is more regular. It uses the word for "the", and this matches the gender and number[6] of what it refers to. It has a comma before it, and the verb goes to the end. For example, *Der Mann, der da ist . . .* (The man who is there . . .) or *Die Frau, die da ist . . .* (The woman who is there. . .). For direct objects, the word for "who(m)/which" is in the accusative case (*Der Mann, den ich gut kenne . . .* – The man who(m) I know well . . .). It is never left out.

Schau! Das ist der Buntstift, der fehlt.

He! Das sind meine Bilder, die du zerreißt.

1 You will find that reflexive verbs sometimes use a different form of *mich*, *dich*, etc. (see page 28). 2 You can also say *Wie spät ist es?* for "What time is it?". 3 Numbers are shown on page 58. 4 "At one (o'clock)" is either *Um eins* or *Um ein Uhr*. 5 "Whom" is better English for the object. 6 Here, "number" means whether it is singular or plural.

Oh! Das muß der Hinweis sein, den wir suchen.

Es ist Tobias Blumenkohl, der das Band durchschneidet.

Wir können heute abend zurückkommen.

Siehst du das alte Foto da?

Und da ist das Zeichen, das sich auf allen seinen Hinweisen befindet.

Gute Idee!

Speech bubble key

- *Warum versteckt ihr euch?* Why are you hiding?
- *Wir gehen nicht gern in die Schule.* We don't like school.
- *Wieviel Uhr ist es?* What's the time?
- *Es ist acht Uhr, Frau Meyer.* It's eight o'clock, Mrs Meyer.
- *Und jetzt?* And now?
- *Es ist Viertel nach neun.* It's quarter past nine.
- *Kurt, um wieviel Uhr wäschst du dich vormittags?* Kurt, what time do you have a wash in the morning?
- *Um halb acht.* At half past seven.
- *Ziehst du dich ganz allein an?* Do you get dressed all on your own?
- *Ja, natürlich.* Yes, of course.
- *Ich fühle mich nicht sehr wohl.* I don't feel very well.
- *Also, beruhigt euch!* Right, calm down!
- *Schau! Das ist der Buntstift, der fehlt.* Look! That's the crayon that's missing.
- *He! Das sind meine Bilder, die du zerreißt.* Hey! Those are my pictures (that) you're tearing up.
- *Oh! Das muß der Hinweis sein, den wir suchen.* Oh! That must be the clue (that) we're looking for.
- *Siehst du das alte Foto da?* Do you see that old photo there?
- *Es ist Tobias Blumenkohl, der das Band durchschneidet.* That's Tobias Blumenkohl (who's) cutting the ribbon.
- *Und da ist das Zeichen, das sich auf allen seinen Hinweisen befindet.* And there's the sign that's on all his clues.
- *Wir können heute abend zurückkommen.* We can come back this evening.
- *Gute Idee!* Good idea!

New words

der Tagesablauf	(events of the) day[7]
der Buntstift(e)	crayon
das Band(¨er)	ribbon
das Zeichen(-)	sign
die Idee(n)	idea
die Postkarte(n)	postcard
sich rasieren	to shave
sich ärgern	to be/get annoyed
sich verstecken	to hide (yourself)
sich anziehen	to get dressed
sich (wohl) fühlen	to feel (well, happy)
sich beruhigen	to calm down
fehlen	to be missing
zerreißen	to tear up
(durch)schneiden	to cut (through)
sich befinden	to be, to be found/situated
zurückkommen	to come back
sich amüsieren	to enjoy yourself, to have fun/a good time
benutzen	to use
aufwachen	to wake up
sich ausruhen	to have a rest, to relax
vormittags, morgens	in the morning
ganz allein	all alone
natürlich	of course, naturally
heute abend	this evening
alle	all
erst	not until, only (for time or age)

A postcard from Tanja

While they wait for school to end so they can take a closer look at the old photo, Tanja writes a postcard home. Read it and see if you can answer the questions. (Give full sentence answers in German.)

Liebe Mutti,

Wir amüsieren uns hier sehr. Das Blumenkohl-Haus ist toll, und Monikas Eltern sind sehr nett. Sie haben auch einen netten Untermieter, der Dieter heißt, einen Hund und eine Katze und Nachbarn, die eine Ziege haben. Sie haben auch alte Fahrräder, die wir benutzen dürfen. Wir schlafen in unseren Zelten im Garten, aber wir essen und waschen uns im Haus. Ich fühle mich sehr wohl in meinem Zelt. Ich wache schon um sechs Uhr morgens auf (die Sonne scheint und die Vögel singen . . .), aber Erich wacht erst um acht Uhr auf. Er ruht sich gern aus! Magst Du diese Ansichtskarte? Alterhaven ist eine kleine, alte Stadt, die mir gefällt.

Deine Tanja

Frau Mülle[r]
Domstraße
8 München

Wer hat eine Ziege?
Wer ist Dieter?
Was dürfen Tanja und Erich benutzen?

Um wieviel Uhr wacht Erich auf?
Wo essen und waschen sich Erich und Tanja?
Wie heißt die kleine Stadt, die Tanja gefällt?

---

7 *Der Tag(e)* is the usual word for "day".

"To do", "because" and word order

German has two verbs for "to do": *machen* and *tun*. In most cases you can use either, though *machen* is more common. *Machen* also means "to make", and *tun* has other meanings too, such as "to put". *Machen* is regular, but *tun* is slightly irregular. Its present tense is shown here (the *ich* form is often used without its "e" ending).

Tun (to do)

ich tu(e)	I do (am doing)
du tust	you do
er/sie/es tut	he/she/it does
wir tun	we do
ihr tut	you do
sie tun	they do
Sie tun	you do

Was tun Sie hier? Reparieren Sie das Fotokopiergerät?

Äh, ja, das mache ich. Ich bin Mechaniker.[1]

Also, geht's jetzt?

Äh, ja.

Ja . . . ich verpacke eben ein kaputtes Teil.

Kann ich zumachen, Herr Streng?

Ja, natürlich.

Weil (because)

Weil means "because", for example *Ich bleibe hier, weil ich müde bin* (I'm staying here because I'm tired). In German, when a clause (a bit of sentence with its own verb – see page 5) begins with a word like *weil*, the verb goes last. If the clause comes second (as in the example), a comma goes before it. With a modal verb and an infinitive, the modal verb goes last (*Weil ich nicht bleiben kann* – Because I can't stay).

Um . . . zu (to, in order to)

This is used in sentences like "I'm staying here (in order) to help Erich": *Ich bleibe hier, um Erich zu helfen*. In the clause beginning with *um*, the verb (always infinitive) goes at the end, just after *zu*.[2]

Na, wie kommen wir hinein?

Kommt schon!

Was machst du, Tanja?

Sei nicht dumm . . .

Ich suche das Foto, weil es nicht mehr an der Wand ist.

Zu spät! Der Mann mit der Glatze hat schon den Hinweis.

Woher weißt du das?

Weil das da seine Aktentasche ist.

Na schön, wir gehen zur Polizeiwache, um die Tasche abzugeben.

More about German word order

German can use English-style word order (*Er trinkt Tee zum Frühstück* – He drinks tea for breakfast). However it is very flexible. It often uses a different word order without this changing the meaning, so you can also say *Zum Frühstück trinkt er Tee*, or *Tee trinkt er zum Frühstück*. The only rule is that if a sentence does not begin with the subject, the subject goes after the verb.[3]

Also remember that in longer sentences with clauses, German usually puts the verb at the end of the clause (*. . ., weil es keine Cola gibt* – because there's no cola).

---

26 **1** When using *sein* with the name of a profession, you normally use the noun on its own without the word tor "a". **2** With a separable verb, *zu* goes after the prefix, e.g. *um Erich vom Bahnhof abzuholen* (to fetch Erich from the station.) **3** Extra little words such as *ja*, *na gut* or *also* do not count. (Pretend they are not there when working out the word order.)

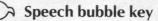

New words

das Fotokopiergerät(e)	photocopier
der Mechaniker(-)	mechanic
das Teil(e)	(spare) part
die Wand(¨e)	wall
das Frühstück(e)	breakfast
die Polizeiwache(n)	police station
der (Polizei)-kommissar(e)	(police) inspector
reparieren	to repair, to mend
verpacken	to wrap (up)
zumachen	to close, to shut
hineinkommen	to come, to get in
bringen	to bring, to take

abgeben* (gibt ab)	to hand in
einkaufen	to do some shopping
arbeiten	to work
gerade, eben	just
kaputt	broken
na	now then, well
nicht mehr	not any more
spät	too late
woher?	where from?, how?
na gut/schön	right, well, OK
dann	then
morgen früh	tomorrow morning
ziemlich	fairly, quite
schwierig	difficult

Mix and match

Here are two sets of six sentences. Each sentence from the first set can be joined to one from the second set using *weil* or *um . . . zu*. Can you work out what the six new sentences are? (You should use *um . . . zu* in the two cases where it is possible. When you do, you have to drop the first two words from the second sentence.)

Wir können nicht kommen.	*Sie will einkaufen.*
Ich nehme dein Fahrrad.	*Es ist sehr schwierig.*
Wir kennen Frau Salbe.	*Ich will nach Alterhaven fahren.*
Sei ruhig! Ich denke gerade nach.	*Sie arbeitet in der Apotheke.*
Sie fährt nach Turmstadt.	*Die Maschine ist kaputt.*
Der Mechaniker ist da.	*Wir essen gerade.*

- *Was tun Sie hier? Reparieren Sie das Fotokopiergerät?* What are you doing here? Are you mending the photocopier?
- *Äh, ja, das mache ich. Ich bin Mechaniker.* Er, yes, I am (doing that). I'm a mechanic.
- *Ja . . . ich verpacke eben ein kaputtes Teil.* Yes, I'm just wrapping up a broken part.
- *Also, geht's jetzt?* So, is it OK now?
- *Äh, ja.* Er, yes.
- *Kann ich zumachen, Herr Streng?* Can I close up, Mr Streng?
- *Ja, natürlich.* Yes, of course.
- *Na, wie kommen wir hinein?* Now then, how do we get in?
- *Kommt schon!* Come this way!
- *Was machst du, Tanja?* What are you doing Tanja?
- *Sei nicht dumm . . .* Don't be stupid . . .
- *Ich suche das Foto, weil es nicht mehr an der Wand ist.* I'm looking for the photo because it's not on the wall any more.
- *Zu spät! Der Mann mit der Glatze hat schon den Hinweis.* Too late! The bald man has already got the clue.
- *Woher weißt du das?* How do you know that?
- *Weil das da seine Aktentasche ist.* Because that's his case there.
- *Na schön, wir gehen zur Polizeiwache, um die Tasche abzugeben.* Right, we're going to the police station to hand in the briefcase.
- *Sie ist zu.* It's closed.
- *Na gut, dann müssen wir morgen früh zurückkommen.* Right, we must come back tomorrow morning.
- *Kennst du den Kommissar?* Do you know the inspector?
- *Ja . . . Er ist ziemlich nett.* Yes . . . He's quite nice.

Personal pronouns

German personal pronouns (words like "I", "you" and so on) have different forms in the various cases. The form you know so far (*ich, du, er*, etc.) is in what is called the nominative case (the case used for the subject – see page 49). The chart on the right shows the pronouns in the nominative, accusative and dative cases, along with their most usual English equivalent.

nominative	accusative	dative
ich (I)	*mich* (me)	*mir* ((to)[1] me)
du (you)	*dich* (you)	*dir* ((to) you)
er (he/it)	*ihn* (him/it)	*ihm* ((to) him/it)
sie (she/it)	*sie* (her/it)	*ihr* ((to) her/it)
es (it)	*es* (it)	*ihm* ((to) it)
wir (we)	*uns* (us)	*uns* ((to) us)
ihr (you)	*euch* (you)	*euch* ((to) you)
sie (they)	*sie* (them)	*ihnen* ((to) them)
Sie (you)	*Sie* (you)	*Ihnen* ((to) you)

More about reflexive verbs

The words used with reflexive verbs (*mich, dich, sich, uns, euch* and *sich* – see page 24), are the same as the accusative personal pronouns, except that *sich* replaces *ihn/sie/es, sie* and *Sie*. There is also a set of dative reflexive pronouns – *mir, dir, sich, uns, euch, sich* – which has the same relationship to the dative personal pronouns. You use these when the reflexive verb has a direct object, for example, to say "I'm washing my face", you say *Ich wasche mir das Gesicht*.

> *Zeigen wir sie deinen Eltern?*

> *Was machen wir mit der Aktentasche?*

> *Nein, wir dürfen sie ihnen nicht zeigen.*

> *Zuerst müssen wir der Polizei alles erzählen.*

> *Ich kann sie in meinem Zelt verstecken.*

> *Das Essen ist fertig!*

> *Gute Idee.*

Summary of cases

Using the right personal pronoun depends on understanding the cases. If your pronoun is the subject, you use the nominative case. Use the accusative case if it is the direct object, and the dative if it is the indirect object. If the personal pronoun is used with a preposition, put it in the case that the preposition requires. There is a genitive case of personal pronouns, but it is hardly ever used nowadays.

Damit, darüber . . .

When in English you have a preposition + "it/them", for example "with it", and this refers to a thing or things (rather than to people or animals), German just adds *da-* to the front of the preposition (*dar-* before a vowel), for example *damit* (with it/them).

After dinner . . .

> *Der Mann mit der Glatze hat den Hinweis aus der Schule.*

> *Um ihn zu finden, müssen wir den Mann mit der Glatze suchen.*

> *Seine Adresse ist vielleicht in seiner Aktentasche.*

> *Setz dich neben mich.*

---

1 The German indirect pronoun already means "to me/you, etc.", so for "He passes the book to me" or ". . . me the book", you just use *mir*.

 Speech bubble key

- *Was machen wir mit der Aktentasche?* What do we do with the briefcase?
- *Zeigen wir sie deinen Eltern?* Do we show it to your parents?
- *Nein, wir dürfen sie ihnen[2] nicht zeigen.* No, we mustn't show it to them.
- *Zuerst müssen wir der Polizei alles erzählen.* First of all we must tell the police everything.
- *Das Essen ist fertig!* Dinner's ready!
- *Ich kann sie in meinem Zelt verstecken.* I can hide it in my tent.
- *Gute Idee.* Good idea.
- *Der Mann mit der Glatze hat den Hinweis aus der Schule.* The bald man's got the clue from the school.
- *Um ihn zu finden, müssen wir den Mann mit der Glatze suchen.* To find it, we have to look for the bald man.
- *Seine Adresse ist vielleicht in seiner Aktentasche.* His address might be[3] in his briefcase.
- *Setz dich neben mich.* You sit next to me.
- *Tanja, reich ihr meine Taschenlampe.* Tanja, pass her my torch.
- *Ein Tagebuch, eine Zeitung...* A diary, a newspaper...
- *Aber schaut darunter... Da sind Papierschnitzel.[4]* But look underneath them... There are some bits of paper...
- *Was ist das?* What's that?
- *Ach, du bist es, Kratzer.* Oh, it's you, Kratzer.
- *Es ist eine zerrissene Postkarte.* It's a torn up postcard.
- *Aber können wir sie noch lesen?* But can we still read it?

The postcard jigsaw

Here are the pieces of postcard that Erich, Tanja and Monika have to put together. Try writing it out with all the bits in the right order, and then work out the meaning of the postcard in English.

mich um ihre Adresse. Dreieich Bauernhof bei Alterhaven. Aber

Herrn Stefan Speck Bahnhofstr. 3 1000 Berlin

Turmstadt ist nicht Jedenfalls, sie haben ein Zimmer frei für sie Dir. Bei ihnen dort schön ruhig.

Lieber Stefan, Vielen Dank für Lothar und Anna der Nähe von

sehr interessant. wahrscheinlich Dich. Ich empfehle ißt man gut und es ist Also, schöne Ferien! Natascha

Hier ist sie: Brückenstraße, warum Turmstadt?

Deinen Brief. Ja, Lauterback wohnen in Turmstadt. Du bittest

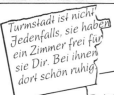

New words

das Gesicht(er)	face	*zeigen*	to show	*vielleicht*	perhaps, maybe
die Polizei	police	*erzählen*	to tell, to talk	*zerrissen*	torn up
die Adresse(n)	address	*verstecken*	to hide	*Herrn[5]*	to Mr
die Taschenlampe(n)	**torch, flashlight**	*finden*	to find	*vielen Dank*	many thanks
das Tagebuch(¨er)	diary	*sich setzen*	to sit down	*jedenfalls*	anyhow
die Zeitung(en)	newspaper	*lesen* (liest)*	to read	*wahrscheinlich*	probably
das Papier(e)	paper	*bitten um*	to ask for	*frei*	free
der/das Schnitzel(-)	bit, scrap	*empfehlen* (empfiehlt)*	to recommend	*ruhig*	quiet
		alles	everything	*schöne Ferien*	(have a) nice holiday/vacation

---

2 If you have both, an accusative personal pronoun always goes before a dative one. **3** *Ist vielleicht* can often translate as "might be" instead of "is perhaps". **4** German can form nouns like this from two nouns. The gender is that of the second one. **5** This is used in written addresses.

Past tenses and adverbs

So far, you have learned verbs in the present tense. From here to page 39, you will learn about past tenses. These are for talking about what happened in the past, for example in English "She did her homework", "She was doing her homework", "She has done her homework". You can see that English has many past tenses. So has German – one of these past tenses is called the imperfect.

The imperfect tense of *haben* and *sein*

The two most useful verbs to learn in the imperfect tense are *haben* and *sein*. For them, the imperfect is the most commonly used past tense.

Haben (imperfect tense)	
ich hatte	I had
du hattest	you had
er/sie/es hatte	he/she/it had
wir hatten	we had
ihr hattet	you had
sie hatten	they had
Sie hatten	you had

Sein (imperfect tense)	
ich war	I was
du warst	you were
er/sie/es war	he/she/it was
wir waren	we were
ihr wart	you were
sie waren	they were
Sie waren	you were

The next morning . . .

Also, wo war diese Aktentasche?

Sie war auf dem Kopiergerät in der Schule.

Und warum wart ihr dort?

Weil wir einen Schatz suchen.

Ja, und in der Schule war ein Hinweis.

Welcher Schatz?

Er gehört meiner Familie.

Ach so, ich verstehe, und dieser Gauner will ihn stehlen.

Adverbs

These are words like "slowly" that add meaning to a verb. There are various types, for instance adverbs of time (that say when something happens), or of manner (how it happens), or of place (where it happens). In German, adverbs may be hard to spot because adjectives can be used as adverbs (*schnell*, for example). Some adverbs are only used as adverbs, though. Quite a few of these end in -*weise*. (You already know some adverbs, for example *jetzt* – now.)

Genau! Der Hinweis ist ein altes Foto.

Gestern abend war das Foto nicht mehr da . . .

aber die Aktentasche vom Gauner war da.

Sie gehört höchstwahrscheinlich dem Lehrer.

Aber nein, der Gauner hatte sie vorher.

Das reicht! Geht jetzt nach Hause.

Useful adverbs

Time
später	later
gestern abend	yesterday evening, last night
heute abend	this evening, tonight
vorher	before(hand)

Manner
genau	exactly (also "exact")
wirklich	really (also "real")

(höchst)-wahrscheinlich	(most) probably
schnell	quickly (also "quick")
(un)glücklicher-weise	(un)luckily, (un)fortunately

Place
dort	there
nach Hause	home[1]
dahin	(to) there

Word order of adverbs

In German, if you use more than one adverb in a sentence, they go in a set order: adverb of time, manner and then place, for example *Er kann später schnell dahin fahren* (He can quickly drive there later). Remember too that words for time often begin sentences, and then the subject follows the verb, for example *Heute abend gehe ich ins Kino* (I'm going to the cinema this evening).[2]

---

[1] You use this with a verb like *gehen* when talking about going home, not being at home. For "at home", you use *zu Hause*.

[2] For more about German word order, see page 26.

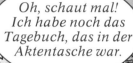

> *Bringen Sie diese Aktentasche schnell zur Schule zurück.*

> *Pech! Wir können ohne die Polizei weitermachen.*

> *Glücklicherweise kennen wir die Adresse von dem Mann mit der Glatze.*

> *Oh, schaut mal! Ich habe noch das Tagebuch, das in der Aktentasche war.*

> *Es war in meiner Tasche.*

New words

die Familie(n)	family	*(So ein) Pech!*	(What) bad luck! Too bad!
der Gauner(-)	crook, scoundrel		
der Lehrer(-)	teacher	*noch*	still
das Restaurant(s)	restaurant	*gemütlich*	cosy, friendly, pleasant
verstehen	to understand, to see	*hübsch*	pretty
stehlen* *(stiehlt)*	to steal	*teuer*	expensive
		gar nicht	not at all
weitermachen	to carry on, to continue		

Speech bubble key

- *Also, wo war diese Aktentasche?* So, where was this briefcase?
- *Sie war auf dem Kopiergerät in der Schule.* It was on the photocopier in the school.
- *Und warum wart ihr dort?* And why were you there?
- *Weil wir einen Schatz suchen.* Because we're looking for treasure.
- *Ja, und in der Schule war ein Hinweis.* Yes, and there was a clue in the school.
- *Welcher Schatz?* What treasure?
- *Er gehört meiner Familie.* It belongs to my family.
- *Ach so, ich verstehe, und dieser Gauner will ihn stehlen.* Aha, I see, and this crook wants to steal it.
- *Genau! Der Hinweis ist ein altes Foto.* Exactly! The clue is an old photo.
- *Gestern abend war das Foto nicht mehr da . . .* The photo wasn't there any more last night . . .
- *aber die Aktentasche vom Gauner war da.* but the crook's briefcase was there.
- *Sie gehört höchstwahrscheinlich dem Lehrer.* It most probably belongs to the teacher.
- *Aber nein, der Gauner hatte sie vorher.* But no, the crook had it before.
- *Das reicht! Geht jetzt nach Hause.* That's enough! Go home now.
- *Bringen Sie diese Aktentasche schnell zur Schule zurück.* Quickly take this briefcase back to the school.
- *Pech! Wir können ohne die Polizei weitermachen.* Too bad! We can carry on without the police.
- *Glücklicherweise kennen wir die Adresse von dem Mann mit der Glatze.* Luckily we know the bald man's address.
- *Oh, schaut mal! Ich habe noch das Tagebuch, das in der Aktentasche war.* Oh, look! I've still got the diary that was in the briefcase!
- *Es war in meiner Tasche.* It was in my pocket.

Picture puzzle

The girl in the pink shirt is showing her friend her holiday photos. Can you match the six things she says with the right photos?

1 *Unser Hotel war klein und gemütlich.*
2 *Es hatte einen großen Garten.*
3 *Der Strand war direkt neben dem Hotel.*
4 *Ich hatte ein sehr hübsches Zimmer.*
5 *Meine Eltern waren wirklich müde.*
6 *Die Restaurants waren gar nicht teuer.*

The imperfect tense

The German imperfect tense has three main uses. Firstly, it is used for things that were happening – where, for example, you would say "he was cycling". Secondly, it is used for something that happened often (He cycled to school every day). Thirdly, it is the proper tense for once-only past events (That morning, he cycled to school). In practice, however, in this last instance German often uses another tense, the perfect. You will find out more about this on page 34.

How to form the imperfect tense

German has two main ways of forming the imperfect. The majority of verbs follow a regular pattern. You take the verb's stem[1] and add a set of imperfect tense endings, as shown here by the imperfect of *holen* (to fetch):

ich holte	I was fetching (fetched)
du holtest	you were fetching
er/sie/es holte	he/she/it was fetching
wir holten	we were fetching
ihr holtet	you were fetching
sie holten	they were fetching
Sie holten	you were fetching

Verbs that work like this are called weak verbs.[2] In the imperfect, the six modal verbs (see page 16) behave like weak verbs but with a few small changes.[3]

Strong verbs

Strong verbs are verbs that have an imperfect tense stem that is different from their present tense stem. You have to learn this.[4] The *ich* and *er* forms add no endings, the rest add the endings shown here by the imperfect of *singen*:

ich sang	I was singing (sang)
du sangst	you were singing
er/sie/es sang	he/she/it was singing
wir sangen	we were singing
ihr sangt	you were singing
sie sangen	they were singing
Sie sangen	you were singing

Mixed verbs

German has a few mixed verbs, which you have to learn. These have a change in the stem like strong verbs, but take the weak verb endings. The three most useful ones are *bringen* (imperfect *ich/er* forms: *brachte*), *denken* (*dachte*) and *wissen* (*wußte*).

Was ist das?

Es war im Tagebuch.

Es sieht interessant aus . . .

Rare Vögel der Rarafugal-Inseln

Vor hundert Jahren gab es viele blaue Papageien auf den Rarafugal-Inseln. Die Einwohner beteten sie an und bauten Tempel ihnen zu Ehren.

Diese Vögel findet man nun sehr selten, und man darf sie nicht fangen. Letztes Jahr konnte man hin und wieder ein paar auf einer entlegenen verlassenen Insel namens Kuckuck sehen.

Herr Speck,
Besorgen Sie mir ein Paar blaue Papageien für meine Sammlung.
Ihr Lohn: 100 000 Mark.

Frau Eule

1 Remember: the stem is the infinitive minus "(e)n". 2 Weak verbs with a stem ending in "d" or "t" add "e" to their stem in the imperfect, e.g. *ich arbeitete* (I worked) from *arbeiten*. 3 *Müssen, mögen, können* and *dürfen* lose the umlaut, the "g" of

> *Mensch! Die Rarafugal-Inseln . . . Mein Urgroßvater ging oft dahin, um die Pflanzen anzusehen.*

> *Er war Botaniker.*

> *Und der Mann mit der Glatze war auf dieser Inselgruppe, um Papageien zu stehlen.*

> *Kommt schon. Ich will euch etwas zu Hause zeigen.*

New words

das Jahr(e)	year
der Papagei(en)	parrot
der Einwohner(-)	inhabitant
der Tempel(-)	temple
das Paar(e)	pair
die Sammlung(en)	collection
der Lohn(¨e)	wage, fee
die Mark(-)	mark[5]
die Pflanze(n)	plant
der Botaniker(-)	botanist
die Inselgruppe(n)	(group of) islands
das Verschwinden	disappearance
der Kollege(n)	colleague, fellow-
das Boot(e)	boat
die Sturmzeit(en)	stormy season
der Gouverneur(e)	governor
denken	to think
aussehen* (sieht aus)	to seem, to look
anbeten	to worship
bauen	to build
fangen* (fängt)	to catch
besorgen	to get, to acquire
dahingehen	to go there
ansehen* (sieht an)	to look at
herrschen	to be (for weather)
rar	rare, scarce
vor [+ dat]	ago
[dat +] zu Ehren	in . . .'s honour
nun	now
selten	rare(ly), seldom
der/die/das letzte(n)	the last
hin und wieder	now and again
ein paar	a few
entlegen	remote, isolated
namens	called
Mensch!	Hey!, Wow!, Man!
sehr geehrter	dear (formal)
leider	unfortunately
wahrscheinlich	probably
tot	dead
zur Zeit	at the time
gefährlich	dangerous
(zusammen) mit	(together) with

🗨 Speech bubble key

- *Was ist das?* What's that?
- *Es war im Tagebuch.* It was in the diary.
- *Es sieht interessant aus . . .* It looks interesting . . .
- **The magazine cutting:** Rare birds of the Rarafugal islands
A hundred years ago, there were many blue parrots in the Rarafugal islands. The inhabitants worshipped them and built temples in their honour. You very rarely find these birds now and you are not allowed to catch them. Last year you could see a few every now and again on a remote desert island called Kuckuck.
- **The message:** Mr Speck,
Get me a pair of blue parrots for my collection. Your fee: 100,000 Marks. Mrs Eule
- *Mensch! Die Rarafugal-Inseln . . . Mein Urgroßvater ging oft dahin, um die Pflanzen anzusehen.* Hey! The Rarafugal Islands . . . My great-grandfather often went there to look at the plants.
- *Er war Botaniker.* He was a botanist.
- *Und der Mann mit der Glatze war auf dieser Inselgruppe, um Papageien zu stehlen.* And the bald man was on those islands to steal some parrots.
- *Kommt schon. Ich will euch etwas zu Hause zeigen.* Come on. I want to show you something at home.

Tobias Blumenkohl's disappearance

Back at home, Tanja shows her friends an old letter addressed to her grandfather, Georg. To find out what it says, read it and translate it into English.

Sehr geehrter Herr,   *Rarafugalstadt*
Leider ist Ihr Vater wahrscheinlich tot. Er kannte unsere Inseln gut, aber zur Zeit seines Verschwindens suchte er Pflanzen auf gefährlichen, entlegenen Inseln. Er arbeitete mit zwei Kollegen zusammen. Sie hatten ein gutes Boot, aber es herrschte die Sturmzeit.
Pedro Peperoni
Gouverneur der Rarafugal-Inseln

mögen becomes "ch" and the "ss" of *müssen* becomes ß. **4** There is a list of the most common strong verbs on page 52. It shows the imperfect stems. **5** This is German money.

The perfect tense

The perfect tense is the tense that is most used in everyday German for one-off past events (such as "They visited her yesterday"). Formal, written German mostly uses the imperfect for such events. In practice, everyday German also mixes in a few verbs in the imperfect, so there is no clear rule about this. However, the perfect is very common in everyday conversations and informal letters.

How to form the perfect tense

The perfect tense is made of two bits – the present tense of *haben* (or sometimes *sein*), plus a special form of the verb you are using, called the past participle. For example, the perfect tense *ich* form of *lachen* is *ich habe gelacht* (I laughed). The past participle goes to the end of the sentence. There is more about verbs that form the perfect with *sein* on page 36.

The past participle of weak verbs

It is easy to form the past participle of weak verbs (verbs that follow a regular pattern in the imperfect – see page 32). The stem usually adds "ge" on the front and "t" on the end, so for *machen* it is *gemacht*.[1]

The past participle of strong verbs

The past participle of strong verbs (see page 32) also usually begins with "ge", but it ends with "en", and these add on to a perfect tense stem that is not always the same as the imperfect stem. For example, the imperfect of *singen* is *ich sang*, but the perfect is *ich habe gesungen*. You have to learn the past participles of strong verbs. A few are shown below:[2]

essen, gegessen   stehlen, gestohlen
finden, gefunden   treffen, getroffen
geben, gegeben   vergessen, vergessen
sehen, gesehen   verlieren, verloren
stehen, gestanden

Mixed verbs

Mixed verbs have the same stem in the perfect as in the imperfect (see page 32). For the past participle, add "ge" and "t" as for weak verbs.

New words

das Mittagessen(-)	lunch	*geben* (gibt)*	to give
das Brot(e)	bread, loaf	*vergessen*(vergißt)*	to forget
der Eingang(¨e)	entrance	*mitbringen*	to bring (along) with you
die Kiste(n)	chest, case, crate		
der Tisch(e)	table	*warten*	to wait
die Sitzung(en)	meeting	*regnen*	to rain
der Schlüssel(-)	key	*einstellen*	to put away/in (the proper place)
die Hosentasche(n)	trouser pocket		
der Inhaber(-)	proprietor, owner	*legen*	to put
der Geldschrank(¨e)	safe	*schaffen*	to manage
		erreichen	to reach
		treffen* (trifft)	to meet
lachen	to laugh	*verlieren*	to lose

sagen	to say
Glück haben	to be lucky
das macht nichts	it doesn't matter
Vati	Dad(dy)
rostig	rusty
innen drin	inside
lang	long
davon	about it
überall	everywhere
danke schön	thank you (very much)
gestern	yesterday
umsonst	(for) free
heute	today

1 In separable verbs, the "ge" goes between the prefix and the verb proper, e.g. *eingestellt* (from *einstellen*). There are also a few verbs that do not add "ge" (verbs ending in "ieren" and verbs with an inseparable prefix like *be-*, *er-* and *ver-*). **2** These examples all form their perfect with *haben*. See page 52 for a longer list of strong verbs.

💬 **Speech bubble key**

●*Das Mittagessen ist fast fertig!* Lunch is nearly ready!
● *Habt ihr Brot mitgebracht?* Did you bring any bread back with you?
●*O Entschuldigung, das haben wir vergessen.* Oh sorry, we forgot.
●*Das macht nichts.* It doesn't matter.
●*Wir müssen auf Vati warten. Er kommt gleich.* We have to wait for Dad. He's on his way.
●*Monika, die Fahrräder! Es regnet . . .* Monika, the bicycles! It's raining . . .
●*Es ist ja gut. Wir haben sie schon eingestellt.* It's OK. We've already put them away.
●*Hast du das Tagebuch?* Have you got the diary?
●*Nein, ich habe es in mein Zelt gelegt. Bleibt hier!* No, I put it in my tent. Wait here!
●*Ach . . . Hier erklärt er, wie er Tobias Blumenkohls Brief gefunden hat.* Oh . . . Here he explains how he found Tobias Blumenkohl's letter.
●*Er suchte blaue Papageien . . .* He was looking for blue parrots . . .
●*Er hat es geschafft, Kuckuck-Insel zu erreichen.* He managed to get to Kuckuck Island.
●*Am Eingang zu einer Höhle hat er eine rostige, alte Kiste gesehen.* At the entrance to a cave he saw a rusty old chest.
●*Innen drin hat er einen Brief gefunden, der von einem Schatz sprach.* Inside, he found a letter that talked about treasure.
●*Ja, das war der Brief, den er gestohlen hat.* Yes, that was the letter he stole.
●*Zu Tisch! Hier kommt Vati.* Come to the table! Here comes Dad.
●*Entschuldigung, ich habe eine sehr lange Sitzung gehabt.* Sorry, I had a very long meeting.

Using past tenses

Try completing the story below by putting the verbs in brackets in the perfect tense (any strong verbs you will need are shown on the page opposite).

Zwei Freunde, Freddi und Ali, wollten Jeans kaufen und gingen in die Stadt. Später erzählte Freddi seiner Mutter davon: "Ich (.....) Ali in der Stadt (treffen). Wir (.....) überall gute Jeans (suchen). In einem Geschäft (.....) wir zwei Schlüssel in einer Hosentasche (finden) und wir (.....) sie dem Inhaber (geben). Er sagte: "Die Schlüssel zu meinem Geldschrank! Danke schön! Gestern (.....) ich sie (verlieren). Ich (.....) sie überall (suchen), aber ich konnte sie nicht finden." Und dann (.....) er uns die Jeans umsonst (geben)! Wir (.....) heute Glück (haben)!"

35

The perfect tense with *sein*

The perfect tense of certain verbs is formed with the present tense of *sein*, not *haben*, for example *Ich bin gegangen* (I went). Some of the most useful of these *sein* verbs are shown in the two lists below, with their past participles in brackets.

Weak *sein* verbs

aufwachen (aufgewacht)[1]	to wake up
begegnen (begegnet)[2]	to meet (bump into)
folgen (gefolgt)	to follow
klettern (geklettert)	to climb, to clamber
passieren (passiert)	to happen
stürzen (gestürzt)	to fall, to plunge

Strong *sein* verbs

ankommen (angekommen)	to arrive	*gelingen (gelungen)*	to succeed
aufstehen (aufgestanden)	to get up	*geschehen (geschehen)*	to happen
		kommen (gekommen)	to come
bleiben (geblieben)	to stay	*sein (gewesen)*	to be
erscheinen (erschienen)	to appear, to seem	*laufen (gelaufen)*	to run, to walk
fahren (gefahren)	to go, to drive	*schwimmen (geschwommen)*	to swim
fallen (gefallen)	to fall	*steigen (gestiegen)*	to climb, to go up
fliegen (geflogen)	to fly	*sterben (gestorben)*	to die
gehen (gegangen)	to go, to walk	*werden (geworden)*	to become

Speech bubble key

- *Wir müssen zum Dreieich-Bauernhof gehen,* We must go to Dreieich farm,
- *...um den Mann mit der Glatze und den Hinweis aus der Schule zu suchen. ...*to look for the bald man and the clue from the school.
- *Kaffee, Herr Speck?* Coffee, Mr Speck?

- *Danke schön... Äh, ich wollte Sie etwas fragen.* Thank you... Er, I wanted to ask you something.
- *Heute morgen bin ich nach Turmstadt gefahren.* I went to Turmstadt this morning.
- *Ich habe das Schloß und die zwei Türme gesehen,* I saw the castle and the two towers,

- *aber den zerstörten Turm habe ich nicht gefunden.* but I didn't find the ruined tower.
- *Warum wollen Sie den*[3] *sehen? Es sind nur alte Steine.* Why do you want to see it? It's only old stones.
- *Äh... ich mag Ruinen.* Er... I like ruins.
- *Na, sind Sie in den Park gegangen?*

---

1 Remember, "ge" goes after the prefix in separable verbs. **2** Remember that some verbs do not add "ge". **3** Note that in spoken German, the appropriate case of *der/die/das* (the) is often used to mean "he", "she", "it", etc.

How to spot a *sein* verb

Notice how most verbs that form the perfect tense with *sein* involve a change of place or state, for example *fallen* (to fall) or *sterben* (to die).

Learning tip

With each new verb, try to learn the infinitive and the *er* forms of the present, imperfect and perfect tenses, such as *gehen, geht, ging, ist gegangen*. The present tense *er* form tells you if the verb is irregular in the present. The imperfect tense *er* form tells you if it is a strong verb, and if so, what its imperfect stem is. The perfect gives you its past participle and tells you whether it is a *haben* or a *sein* verb.

New words

der Kaffee	coffee
der Stein(e)	stone, rock
die Ruine(n)	ruin
der Park(s)	park
das Kalb("er)	calf
das Bett(en)	bed
das Fenster (-)	window
fragen	to ask
hinuntergehen	to go down
etwas	something
heute morgen	this morning
zerstört	destroyed, ruined
nur	only
heute nacht	last night, tonight
schön	lovely, beautiful
es geht ihnen gut	they're fine

Say it in German

Put these sentences into German. The verbs must go into the perfect tense, but some form the perfect with *haben* and some with *sein*.

Mr Speck looked for the old tower but he didn't find it.
Tanja, Erich and Monika went to the farm.
They found him.
Mr Speck didn't see them.
Tanja and Monika hid under the window.

Well, did you go to the park?
●*Ja, aber ich habe dort nichts gesehen.* Yes, but I didn't see anything there.
●*Aha, Sie sind nicht bis zum Fluß hinuntergegangen.* Ah, you didn't go down to the river.
●*Ja, Butterblume hat heute nacht ein schönes Kalb bekommen.*[4] Yes, Butterblume had a lovely calf last night.
●*Ich bin um zwei Uhr morgens ins Bett gegangen!* I went to bed at two in the morning!
●*Ja, es geht ihnen gut.* Yes they're well.
●*Ich bin heute morgen zu ihnen gegangen.* I went to (see) them this morning.
●*...Ja, der alte Turm ist am Fluß.* ...Yes, the old tower is by the river.
●*Ach, wirklich? Das ist sehr interessant.* Oh, really? That's very interesting.
●*Der nächste Hinweis muß im alten Turm sein.* The next clue must be in the old tower.

---

4 *Bekommen* (to receive, to get) is also used for "to have (babies/offspring)".

More about the perfect tense

Like German, English has a perfect tense. This is made from "to have" and the past participle, for example "He has eaten". Normally, where you use the perfect in English, you also use it in German, so you say *Er hat gegessen*. As you can see, *er hat gegessen* can either mean "he ate" (see page 34) or "he has eaten".

More about the past participle

In English, the past participle can be used on its own like an adjective, for example "stolen papers". German can do the same thing, but the participle then behaves exactly like an adjective and agrees with the noun it is used with, for example *gestohlene Papiere* (stolen papers).

Er hat also den Hinweis aus der Schule entziffert,...

Aber er hat ihn noch nicht gefunden.

und das hat ihn zum alten Turm geschickt.

Wir müssen also sofort dahin[1] – vor ihm.

Wir sind zurückgekommen, um unsere Fahrräder zu holen.

Guten Tag. Können Sie dieses beschädigte Ohr reparieren?

"Mine", "yours", "his", etc.

To say "mine", "yours", "his" and so on, German mostly uses a special set of words (see right). These change to match the noun they are replacing, for example, talking about a bag (*eine Tasche*), you say *Meine ist blau* (Mine is blue).

German has other words for "mine", "yours" and so on, but those shown on the right are the most common. Also, remember that German often uses *gehören* for saying whose something is (see page 12), for instance *Das gehört mir* (It's mine – word for word, "It belongs to me...").

(m)	(f)	(n)	(pl)	
meiner	meine	mein(e)s	meine	mine
deiner	deine	dein(e)s	deine	yours
seiner	seine	sein(e)s	seine	his/its
ihrer	ihre	ihr(e)s	ihre	hers/its
uns(e)rer	uns(e)re	unser(e)s	uns(e)re	ours
eu(e)rer	eu(e)re	euer(e)s	eu(e)re	yours
ihrer	ihre	ihr(e)s	ihre	theirs
Ihrer	Ihre	Ihr(e)s	Ihre	yours

Wegen dem Zaun habe ich den Turm nie richtig erforscht.

Wem gehört diese Mütze?

Sie gehört ihm!

1 After a modal verb such as *müssen*, you often leave out the infinitive verb if it is a verb of movement (e.g. *gehen* or *kommen*).

New words

das Ohr(en)	ear	*erforschen*	to explore
der Zaun(¨e)	fence	*untersuchen*	to examine
die Mütze(n)	cap	*erhalten* (erhält)*	to preserve,
das Denkmal(¨er)	monument		to maintain, to
der Pirat(en)	pirate		keep
die Rache	revenge	*zerstören*	to destroy
der Kampf(¨e)	battle	*vertreiben*	to expel, to drive out
die Festung(en)	fort, fortress	*verschwinden*	to disappear
das Land(¨er)	country, land		
		noch nicht	not yet
entziffern	to decipher,	*sofort*	straight away
	to work out	*wegen* (+ gen or	because of
schicken	to send	dat)	
dahingehen	to go there	*nie(mals)*	never
zurückkommen	to come back	*das stimmt*	that's right/true
holen	to fetch	*überall*	everywhere
beschädigen	to damage	*als*	as (a)

Speech bubble key

● *Er hat also den Hinweis aus der Schule entziffert,...* So, he's worked out the clue from the school...

● *und das hat ihn zum alten Turm geschickt.* and that sent him to the old tower.

● *Aber er hat ihn noch nicht gefunden.* But he hasn't found it yet.

● *Wir müssen also sofort dahin[1] – vor ihm.* So we must go there straight away – before him.

● *Wir sind zurückgekommen, um unsere Fahrräder zu holen.* We've come back to fetch our bikes.

● *Guten Tag. Können Sie dieses beschädigte Ohr reparieren?* Hello. Can you mend this damaged ear?

● *Wegen dem Zaun habe ich den Turm nie richtig erforscht.* I've never really explored the tower properly because of the fence.

● *Wem gehört diese Mütze?* Whose cap is this?

● *Sie gehört ihm!* It's his!

● *Aber nein, er hat schon seine.* No it's not, he's got his.

● *Schau mal! Deine hast du nicht mehr!* Look! You haven't got yours any more!

● *Ach ja, das stimmt.* Oh yes, that's true.

● *Nichts! Ich hab' überall gesucht und jeden Stein untersucht.* Nothing! I've looked everywhere and examined each stone.

● *Mensch! Ich hab' hier etwas gefunden.* Hey! I've found something here.

● *Schaut! Das ist Tobias Blumenkohls Zeichen!* Look! It's Tobias Blumenkohl's sign!

The writing on the tower

Tobias Blumenkohl put his sign on an old plaque. This is what Tanja, Erich and Monika see when they clear away the ivy. It gives them a good idea of where to go next. Translate it and see what you think.

> Wir haben diesen alten Turm als Denkmal für die Einwohner von Turmstadt erhalten.
>
> Vor drei Jahren haben ihn die Piraten von der Pirateninsel zerstört, aber jetzt haben wir unsere Rache bekommen. Wir haben nun unseren letzten Kampf gegen sie gewonnen. Wir haben sie aus ihrer Festung auf der Insel vertrieben, und sie sind aus unserem Land verschwunden.

2 In spoken German, you often drop the "e" like this from the end of a verb's *ich* form.

The future tense

To talk about future events, English normally uses its future tense (We will/We'll sing/be singing), or "going to" + a verb (We're going to sing). German also has a future tense. In theory, you can nearly always use this where English uses its future tense or its "going to" future. In practice, though, German only uses its future tense occasionally and mostly just uses the present tense (there is more about this on page 42).

How to form the future tense

The German future tense is easy to form. For all verbs, you use the present tense of the verb *werden* (to become) + the infinitive of the verb you are using[1] (see the future tense of *singen* below on the left). Notice that *werden* is an irregular verb.

Singen (future tense)

ich werde singen	I will sing
du wirst singen	you will sing
er/sie/es wird singen	he/she/it will sing
wir werden singen	we will sing
ihr werdet singen	you will sing
sie werden singen	they will sing
Sie werden singen	you will sing

More about *werden*

Remember that although *werden* is used to form the future tense, it is also often used on its own just to mean "to become", for example *Ich werde müde* (I'm becoming/getting tired). Note that English often uses "get" to mean "become", for example "It's getting dark", or "They're getting silly", so in these cases you must use *werden* and say *Es wird dunkel, Sie werden dumm*.

Beware: *werden* means "to become, to get", but *bekommen* means "to receive, to get" – it does not mean "to become".

New words

die Überfahrt(en)	(sea) crossing
die Nacht(¨e)	night
das Laub [no pl]	leaves, foliage
die Spur(en)	trail, track
die Richtung(en)	direction
der Zettel(-)	note
das Versteck(e)	hiding-place
die Erde	earth, soil, world
die Aufgabe(n)	task
das Gitter(-)	grid, bars
das Juwel(en)	jewel
das Vermögen(-)	fortune
werden* (wird)	to become
verdecken	to cover, to hide
hinterlassen* (hinterläßt)	to leave behind
dalassen* (läßt da)	to leave here/there
beschmutzen	to dirty
aussehen* (sieht aus)	to look, to seem
setzen	to put
hereinfallen* auf [+ acc] (fällt auf ... herein)	to fall for
hineingehen	to go, to come in
es geht nicht	it's no good, it won't work
dunkel	dark
gefährlich	dangerous
während [+ gen]	during
so	like this/that
falsch	false, wrong
großartig	brilliant, terrific
Keine Sorge!	Don't worry!
perfekt	perfect
bestimmt	definitely
ohne	without
auf diese Weise	(in) this way
drinnen	inside
mit Holzplatten verkleidet	with wooden panels

> Also, wir müssen zur Pirateninsel fahren.

> Es wird schon dunkel und die Überfahrt wird gefährlich sein.

> Wir werden doch zu spät ankommen. Heute geht's nicht.

> Aber hier wird der Mann den Hinweis finden und ...

> Also, dann müssen wir diesen Hinweis mit Laub verdecken. So!

> er wird vielleicht während der Nacht zur Insel fahren.

> Wir können auch eine falsche Spur hinterlassen.

> Großartig! Er wird in die falsche Richtung gehen ...

> und uns nicht stören.

1 If you use a modal verb in the future tense with another verb in the infinitive, the modal infinitive goes last, e.g. *Ich werde singen können* (I'll be able to sing).

A few minutes later . . .

The false trail

This is Monika's note. She has used funny writing. To discover where she is sending the bald man, you will have to work out how to read it. Then you can translate it into English.

B.T. lhow beL. nednif negömreV niem dnu nelewuJ eniem ella uD tsriw troD. nehes dnaW etedielkrev nettalpzloH tim enie uD tsriw nennirD. nehegnienih uD tsriw esieW eseid fuA. nehes rettiG enho retsneF nie uD tsriw troD. nessüm neheg nevahretlA ni ehcawieziloP ruz tsriw uD. nies gireiwhcs driw eiS. ebagfuA etztel enieD tsi reiH. nednufeg, ebah nessalretnih hci eid, esiewniH ella uD tsah nun, nhoS rebeil nieM.

Speech bubble key

- *Also, wir müssen zur Pirateninsel fahren.* So, we must go to Pirates' Island.
- *Wir werden doch zu spät ankommen. Heute geht's nicht.* But we'll get there too late. Today's no good.
- *Es wird schon dunkel und die Überfahrt wird gefährlich sein.* It's already getting dark and the crossing will be dangerous.
- *Aber hier wird der Mann den Hinweis finden und . . .* But the man will find the clue here and . . .
- *er wird vielleicht während der Nacht zur Insel fahren.* he might[2] go to the island during the night.
- *Also, dann müssen wir diesen Hinweis mit Laub verdecken. So!* Well then, we must hide this clue with leaves. There!
- *Wir können auch eine falsche Spur hinterlassen.* We can also leave a false trail.
- *Großartig! Er wird in die falsche Richtung gehen . . .* Brilliant! He'll go in the wrong direction . . .
- *und uns nicht stören.* and won't[3] disturb us.
- *Na gut, wir müssen ihm einen Zettel dalassen.* Right, we must leave him a note here.
- *Ich habe eine gute Idee.* I've got a good idea.
- *Aber wo werden wir ihn verstecken?* But where shall[4] we hide it?
- *Erich und ich können ein gutes Versteck suchen.* Erich and I can look for a good hiding-place.
- *Du wirst den Zettel mit Erde beschmutzen müssen.* You'll have to dirty the note with some soil.
- *Ja, ja, keine Sorge! Er wird perfekt aussehen.* Yes, don't worry! It's going to look perfect.
- *Wir können ihn hier verstecken und sein Zeichen darauf setzen.* We can hide it here and put his sign on there.
- *Das ist wirklich großartig! Darauf wird er bestimmt hereinfallen.* That's really brilliant! He'll definitely fall for it.

2 Notice that *er wird vielleicht* (he will perhaps) is best translated as "he might". 3 Note that "will not" turns into "won't".
4 "Shall" can be used in English instead of "will" in the "I" and "we" forms, especially in questions.

More about the future

Apart from the future tense, German has another way of talking about the future. This is simply to use the present tense, for example *Ich bin bald fertig* (I'll be ready soon). Both spoken German and more formal, written German do this a lot.

There is no rule about when to use which tense.

However, in sentences like the one on the left which are clearly about events in the future, the present tense is far more common than the future tense. Note that informal English can sometimes work in the same way, for example "I'm driving to Hamburg tomorrow" – *Morgen fahre ich nach Hamburg*.

Zu (to) + infinitive verbs

In English, if you use a main verb followed by an infinitive verb, the infinitive usually has "to" before it (I want to know). However, if the main verb is one of a small set (e.g. "must", "can" or "make") you drop "to" (I must know). German works in a similar way.

You usually need *zu* (to), for example *Er begann zu singen* (He started to sing),[1] but not with certain verbs such as *gehen* or the modal verbs (see page 16), for example *Ich muß wissen* (I must know). Remember that in German the infinitive verb goes to the end.

"This/that one"

The German for "this/that one" is *dieser*, *diese* or *dieses*. For "these/those ones", you say *diese*. These words change like *der*, *die*, *das*, *die* according to the case of whatever they refer to. You can also just use the word for "the" + *hier* (here) or + *da* (there). For example, talking about a clock (*eine Uhr*): *Diese geht nicht richtig*, or *Die da geht nicht richtig* (That one's not working properly).

1 If the infinitive verb is separable, *zu* goes between the prefix and the actual verb.

New words

die Nummer(n)	number
die Einzelheit(en)	detail
die Uhr(en)	clock
die Fensterscheibe(n)	window-pane
leichter Diebstahl [m]	petty theft
die Belohnung(en)	reward
aufräumen	to tidy up
durchfaxen	to fax through
einschlagen* *(schlägt ein)*	to break, to smash in
helfen* [+ dat] *(hilft)*	to help
verhaftet sein	to be under arrest
zurückkommen	to come back
in Ordnung	fine, OK
ein bißchen	a bit/little
(auf) Wiedersehen	goodbye
weiter	further
wirklich	really
(auf) Wiederhören	goodbye (on phone)
endlich	at last
X Jahre alt	X years old
Halt!	stop!

Talking about the future

Here are seven sentences in English for you to translate into German. Use the future tense only where shown.

Susanne will be here. (future tense)

I'll fetch it.

We're going to the cinema tonight.

Will you write to me? (future tense)

Richard will come home soon.

I'll write the letter tomorrow.

They'll bring a cake. (future tense)

2 Notice that in German, you have a comma at the start of the clause with the infinitive verb if this clause is more than just *zu* + infinitive verb. **3** Note that English often says "go and" instead of "go to".

Comparisons are when you say things like "taller" or "the tallest". In English you either make them like this (with "er" or "est"), or, for longer words, with "more" or "the most" (more/the most important). Comparisons are made with either adjectives or adverbs (with most adverbs, you only use "more, the most"), for example, with an adjective, "She's taller/the tallest", or, with an adverb, "It goes more/the most often".

Comparisons with adjectives

In German, to say "-er" or "more" with an adjective, you normally add -er to the adjective, and for "-est", "the most", you use *der/die/das* + [adjective + -st]. However you must also remember to add the appropriate endings, so for example, with *klein* (small), you say *ein kleinerer Pulli* (a smaller jumper), but *eine kleinere Jacke* (a smaller jacket), and *der kleinste Pulli* (the smallest jumper), *die kleinste Jacke* (the smallest jacket). Some common short adjectives also add an umlaut when used in a comparison.[1]

"Than" and "as . . . as"

In comparisons, to say "than" as in "He's older than his sister", German uses *als*: *Er ist älter als seine Schwester*.

To say "(just) as . . . as" (for example, "just as tall as"), you use *(genau)so . . . wie* (so you say *genauso groß wie*). You can also use *genauso* on its own – *Sie ist genauso groß* (She's just as tall).

Comparisons with adverbs

Comparisons with adverbs are made by adding -er and with *am* + [adverb + -sten], for example with *langsam* (slowly), you say *langsamer, am langsamsten* (more slowly, the most slowly).[2]

Common exceptions

A few common words do not follow the usual method for comparisons. Here are some useful ones (some also have irregular comparisons in English):

Adjectives With *gut* (good), you say *besser, der beste* (better, the best). With *nah* (near), you say *näher, der nächste* (nearer, the nearest/next). With *viel* (much, many), you say *mehr, der meiste* (more, the most).

Adverbs With *bald* (soon), you say *eher, am ehesten* (sooner, the soonest). With *gern* (gladly), you say *lieber, am liebsten* (more gladly, the most gladly).[3] With *gut* (well), you say *besser, am besten* (better, the best).

44 1 E.g. with *groß* (big, tall), you say *größer, der größte* (taller, the tallest). Other adjectives like this are *alt* (old), *lang* (long) and *kurz* (short). See list, page 50. 2 You will also find that adjectives can be used with *am* + -sten when they are used without a

New words

das Handtuch(¨er)	towel, cloth	drehen	to turn, to go around	der/die/das andere(n)	the other(s)
der Riemen(-)	oar	rudern	to row	im Kreis	in a circle, in circles
der Kerker(-)	dungeon	sich (etwas) anschauen	to (take a) look at (something)	einfach	simply, just
der Tunnel(-)	tunnel			kräftig	strong, powerful
leihen	to lend, to hire			(da)hinunter	down (there)
sich (etwas) leihen	to borrow (something)	naß	wet	komisch	funny, strange, odd
beginnen	to begin, to start	kurz	short	normalerweise	normally
				am Ende [+ gen]	at the end of

Da ist die Festung.

Sie hat viele Kerker und Tunnel,

Sie ist noch älter als der alte Turm.

. . . aber man kann nicht dahinunter.

Komisch. Das Tor ist normalerweise zu.

Ach, Mensch!

Ich gehe lieber nicht hinunter.

Schaut mal, es gibt vier Tunnel.

Oh, nein!

Kommt hierher! Schaut euch das mal an!

Wir können nicht mehr hinaus!

TUNNELS AM ENDE DES LÄNGSTEN

Which is the longest tunnel?

Monika, Erich and Tanja know they must go to the end of the longest tunnel. But which one is it? Using footsteps as a measure (their feet are about the same size), Erich and Monika measure out a tunnel each and Tanja does the other two. This is what they say when they compare measurements:

Mein Tunnel ist nicht so lang wie deiner.

Mein erster Tunnel war genauso lang wie deiner, aber mein zweiter Tunnel ist kürzer.

Meiner ist länger als Tanjas erster Tunnel.

Also, welcher ist der längste Tunnel? `

Can you answer Erich's question? (Give a full answer in German.)

- Du hast den besseren Riemen. You've got the better oar.
- Nein, hab' ich nicht. Ich bin einfach kräftiger als du. No, I haven't. I'm simply stronger than you.
- Da ist die Festung. There's the fort.
- Sie ist noch älter als der alte Turm. It's even older than the old tower.

- Sie hat viele Kerker und Tunnel, It's got lots of dungeons and tunnels,
- . . . aber man kann nicht dahinunter. but you can't (go) down there.
- Komisch. Das Tor ist normalerweise zu. Strange. The gate's normally shut.
- Ich gehe lieber nicht hinunter. I'd rather not go down.

- Ach, Mensch! Oh no!
- Schaut mal, es gibt vier Tunnel. Look, there are four tunnels.
- Oh, nein! Oh no!
- Wir können nicht mehr hinaus! We can't get out any more!
- Kommt hierher! Schaut euch das mal an! Come here! Take a look at this!

---

noun, e.g. Er ist am größten (He is the tallest). **3** Gern is used with haben to mean "to like" (see page 13). In the same way, you can use lieber and am liebsten to mean "to like better, to prefer" and "to like the most".

The conditional

In English, verbs make their conditional form with "would" (or "'d") – "I'd go, but I'm busy". German works in a similar way. You use a form of *werden* + the infinitive of the verb you want. So, for "would go", add *gehen* to *ich würde*,[1] *du würdest*, *er/sie/es würde, wir würden, ihr würdet* or *sie/Sie würden*.

How to say "if"

In German, "if" is *wenn*.[2] Like "if", it goes with different tenses depending on what you are saying. For things you are just imagining, English uses the past tense and the "would" form (If I had lots of money, I'd go to New York) and German uses the

Sein, haben and modal verbs

German also has another "would" form. You need to know it for *sein*, *haben* and modal verbs, as it is more often used for them than the *würde* form. To make it, take the imperfect tense forms (see page 30 for *haben* and *sein*, page 32 for

modal verbs) and add an umlaut to all but *sollen* and *wollen*, for example *ich hätte*. *Sein* changes in a slightly more complicated way, so it goes: *ich wäre, du wärest, er/sie/es wäre, wir wären, ihr wäret, sie/Sie wären*.

"would" form twice (*Wenn ich viel Geld hätte, würde ich nach New York fahren*). Otherwise, English uses the present and future, and so does German: *Wenn ich Zeit habe, werde ich mitkommen* (If I have time, I'll come along).[3]

Wenn der Schatz hier ist, finden wir ihn!

Nichts! Der Tunnel endet hier.

Wäre es besser, wenn du die Taschenlampe hättest?

Ja. Reich sie mir!

Oh! Es gibt hier einen eisernen Ring an der Mauer. Ich ziehe daran.

Mensch!

Being polite

Like in English, the "would" form is often used in German for extra politeness, for example *ich möchte* (I would like), which you learned on page 10, is the "would" form of *ich mag* (I like), and is used to ask for something politely. In a similar way, *ich hätte gern* from *gern haben* (to like) is another polite way of saying "I would like to have".

Guten Tag, ich möchte mit Monika, Erich und Tanja sprechen.

Ich möchte ihnen danken. Sie haben mir geholfen, einen Verbrecher zu schnappen!

Möchten Sie auf sie warten?

Nein, ich werde zurückkommen. Ich möchte Sie nicht stören.

Aber zuerst könnten Sie uns vielleicht die ganze Geschichte erzählen. Wir wissen nichts!

---

46 1 The infinitive goes to the end of the clause, e.g. *Ich würde ins Kino gehen, aber . . .* (I'd go to the cinema, but . . .). **2** *Wenn* can also mean "when" and "whenever" (though with past tense verbs, *als* is normally used for "when"). **3** Remember, though: German often replaces a future with a present tense. So for this, you could also say *Wenn ich Zeit habe, komme ich mit*.

New words

die Zeit(en)	time	*schnappen*	to catch, to nab
der Ring(e)	ring	*zurückgehen*	to go back
die Mauer(n)	wall	*ziehen [an + dat]*	to pull, to give . . . a pull
der Verbrecher(-)	criminal		
die Geschichte(n)	story, history	*vorschieben*	to push (. . .) in front
die Treppe(n)	**steps, staircase**	*kaufen*	to buy
das Licht(er)	light	*ausgeben* (gibt aus)*	to spend (money)
die Spalte(n)	crack		
das Dach(¨er)	roof	*reparieren lassen*	to have/get . . . repaired
Amerika	America		
die Tante(n)	aunt	*viel*	a lot/lots of
das Gold	gold	*eisern*	iron
		Mutti	Mum
enden	to end		

What if?

When the three get back to the Blumenkohl house, Monika asks her Mum what she would do if she suddenly had lots of money. To complete Heidrun's answers, you must put the verbs in brackets into the right form.

> *Mutti, was würdest du tun, wenn du viel Geld hättest?*

> *Ich (ausgeben) alles!*
>
> *Ich (reparieren lassen) das Dach.*
>
> *Du (bekommen) ein neues Fahrrad.*
>
> *Wir (fahren) nach Amerika, um meine Tante zu besuchen.*

> *Also, wir haben Tobias Blumenkohls Schatz gefunden. Es gibt viel Gold!*

> *Also . . . Wir sollten einen Ausgang suchen.*

> *Schaut mal! Licht!*

> *Vielleicht finden wir einen, wenn wir zur Treppe zurückgehen.*

> *Puh!*

> *Tanja, wenn du die großen Steine da vorschiebst, sieht niemand die Spalte.*

> *Jetzt kann ich Ralf neue Riemen kaufen.*

💬 Speech bubble key

●*Wenn der Schatz hier ist, finden wir ihn!* If the treasure's here, we'll find it!
●*Nichts! Der Tunnel endet hier.* Nothing! The tunnel ends here.
●*Wäre es besser, wenn du die Taschenlampe hättest?* Would it be better if you had the torch?
●*Ja. Reich sie mir!* Yes. Pass it to me!
●*Oh! Es gibt hier einen eisernen Ring an der Mauer. Ich ziehe daran.* Oh! There's an iron ring in the wall here. I'm going to give it a pull.
●*Mensch!* Wow!
●*Guten Tag, ich möchte mit Monika, Erich und Tanja sprechen.* Hello, I'd like to talk to Monika, Erich and

Tanja.
●*Ich möchte ihnen danken. Sie haben mir geholfen, einen Verbrecher zu schnappen!* I'd like to thank them. They helped me catch a criminal!
●*Möchten Sie auf sie warten?* Would you like to wait for them?
●*Nein, ich werde zurückkommen. Ich möchte Sie nicht stören.* No, I'll come back. I wouldn't like to disturb you.
●*Aber zuerst könnten Sie uns vielleicht die ganze Geschichte erzählen. Wir wissen nichts!* But first, perhaps you could[4] tell us the story. We don't know anything!

●*Also . . . Wir sollten einen Ausgang suchen.* Right . . . We should[5] look for a way out.
●*Vielleicht finden wir einen, wenn wir zur Treppe zurückgehen.* We might find one if we go back to the steps.
●*Schaut mal! Licht!* Look! Light!
●*Puh!* Phew!
●*Tanja, wenn du die großen Steine da vorschiebst, sieht niemand die Spalte.* Tanja, if you push those rocks in front, nobody'll see the crack.
●*Jetzt kann ich Ralf neue Riemen kaufen.* Now I can buy Ralf some new oars.

---

4 Note: the conditional form of "can" is "could". 5 Note: the conditional form of "must, to have to" is "should".

A letter to read

Here is a letter with a newspaper cutting that Monika sent to Erich and Tanja after they went home to Munich. There is a lot of German for you to read through and make sense of. You can check how well you have done by looking at the English translations on page 57. There are also some useful words for writing a letter in German.

Letter-writing tips

For Tuesday 7th September, you either write *Dienstag, den 7. September* or *den 7. September*, or just *7. September*.[1] For "Dear", you either write *Lieber* + a masculine name or *Liebe* + a feminine name.

A useful way to sign off is *viele Grüße* (it is the equivalent of "best wishes" or "love from"). After this, you add *Dein/Deine* (meaning "your") – or *Euer/Eure* when writing to more than one person.

In your card or letter, the words for "you" or "your(s)" must all be written with a capital first letter, for example *Vielen Dank für Deinen Brief* (Many thanks for your letter).

Montag, den 2. September

Liebe Tanja, lieber Erich,

Hier ist der Artikel aus dem Kurier, der unsere Geschichte erzählt. Er ist großartig! Was macht Ihr mit Eurem Anteil an der Belohnung? Mit meinem werde ich mir einen Kassettenrecorder kaufen. Wenn Eure Mutter einverstanden ist, besuche ich Euch während der Weihnachtsferien. Also, hoffentlich bis bald!

Viele Grüße

Eure
Monika

KURIER

Freitag, den 30. August

Der Schatz der Familie Blumenkohl

Monika Blumenkohl mit ihren Freunden Erich und Tanja Müller und ihrem Hund, Hüpfer.

Stefan Speck, der Dieb von raren Vögeln, der den Blumenkohl-Schatz stehlen wollte.

Der Monat August ist für Monika Blumenkohl und ihre Freunde Erich und Tanja eine spannende Zeit gewesen. Sie haben einen Schatz gefunden und der Polizei geholfen, den Verbrecher Stefan Speck zu fassen.

Vor vielen Jahren starb Monikas Urgroßvater, Tobias, auf einer entlegenen Insel. Er hinterließ eine Kiste. Diese Kiste war neben dem Eingang zu einer Höhle versteckt. Vor einigen Monaten war Speck auf derselben Insel. Dort suchte er sehr seltene Papageien, die er stehlen wollte.

Zufällig stieß er auf die alte Kiste und fand einen Brief von Tobias darin. Dieser Brief war an Monikas Großvater, Georg. Er war der erste Hinweis in einer Schatzsuche und brachte Speck nach Turmstadt, wo er ihn dummerweise verlor. Erich und Tanja, die gerade ankamen, um einige Tage bei ihrer Freundin Monika zu verbringen, fanden ihn. Die drei jungen Leute schafften es, den Schatz (Gold), der in der alten Piratenfestung versteckt war, zu finden, bevor der Verbrecher es tun konnte. Sie haben auch der Polizei geholfen, Speck zu fassen. Die drei Helden haben auch eine Belohnung von 5 000 Mark von der Polizei bekommen. Wir gratulieren!

New words

der Artikel(-)	article	*die Leute* [pl]	people	*gratulieren* [+ dat]	to congratulate (someone)
der Kurier	messenger	*der Held(en)*	hero		
der Anteil(e)	share, portion			*hoffentlich*	I/we hope, with hope
der Kassetten-recorder(-)	cassette recorder	*einverstanden sein*	to agree	*bis bald*	see you soon
die Weihnachtsferien [pl]	Christmas holidays	*fassen*	to catch, to apprehend	*spannend*	exciting
				versteckt	hidden
der Dieb(e)	thief	*stoßen**	to find (by chance), to come across	*zufällig*	by chance
der Monat(e)	month	*auf* [+ acc]		*dummerweise*	stupidly
die Freundin(nen) [f]	friend (girl)	*(stößt auf)*		*jung*	young
		verbringen	to spend (time)	*bevor*	before

---

1 Note that in dates, although you just write *den* + the number and a full stop, in fact you read it as *den ersten/zweiten/dritten*, etc. (the first, second, third, etc.). For more about saying "first, second, third", etc, see page 58. Days of the week and months are also listed on page 58.

German grammar summary

This section brings together and summarizes the main areas of German grammar introduced in this book. It includes lists and tables that are useful for learning from. Remember that basic grammar terms, such as "noun" and "verb", are explained on page 5.

Nouns and *der, die, das*

All German nouns have a gender. They are either masculine, feminine or neuter.

In the singular (when you are talking about one thing, e.g. "tower" rather than the plural "towers"), the word for "the" is *der* before masculine nouns, *die* before feminine nouns and *das* before neuter nouns.

Examples:
der Turm (the tower)
die Insel (the island)
das Dorf (the village)

By learning nouns with *der, die* or *das* in front of them, you will learn their gender.

As you can see, German nouns are always written with a capital first letter.

Nouns and *ein, eine, ein*

The word for "a" (or "an") is *ein* before masculine and neuter nouns and *eine* before feminine nouns, for example:

ein Turm (a tower)
eine Insel (an island)
ein Dorf (a village)

Plural nouns

German nouns have a variety of ways of forming the plural (the plural is when you are talking about more than one, e.g. "towers").

Most nouns make the plural form by adding one or two letters at the end. Some also add an umlaut (¨), and others only add an umlaut. The umlaut always goes over the last "a", "o" or "u" in the noun (although if the last vowels in the noun are "au", the umlaut goes over the "a"). Some nouns stay the same in the plural, and a few have more unusual plurals, for example *der Fluß* (river), *die Flüsse* (rivers).[1]

The plural word for "the" is *die*, whatever the gender.

Examples:
der Turm (the tower) – *die Türme* (the towers)
die Insel (the island) – *die Inseln* (the islands)
das Dorf (the village) – *die Dörfer* (the villages)
der Hafen (the port) – *die Häfen* (the ports)
das Haus (the house) – *die Häuser* (the houses)
der Koffer (the suitcase) – *die Koffer* (the suitcases)

When learning nouns, you have to learn their plural forms. In word lists, the plural is usually shown in brackets at the end of the noun. For example, *der Turm(¨e)* shows the plural is *Türme*. If the noun does not change in the plural, there is a dash in the bracket. For example, *der Koffer(-)* means the plural is *die Koffer*.

Compound nouns

German has a lot of compound nouns, nouns made up of two or more shorter nouns joined together. Their gender is always that of the last noun, and so is their plural ending, for example, *die Fensterscheibe(n)* (windowpane) is made from *das Fenster* (window) and *die Scheibe* (slice, pane).

The four cases

Nouns and pronouns go into different cases depending on the job they are doing in the sentence. For nouns, this largely means that the words that go with them (such as the words for "the" and "a") change according to the case. With pronouns, the pronouns themselves change (see page 50, bottom of centre column). German has four cases.

The nominative case The case that the noun (or pronoun) is in when it is the subject of a sentence. In word lists, nouns are given in the nominative case.

The accusative case The case that the noun (or pronoun) is in when it is the direct object in a sentence. The accusative is also used after certain prepositions (see below right).

The genitive case The case the noun (or pronoun) goes into to show whose something is. The genitive is also used after a few prepositions (see below right).

The dative case The case used when the noun (or pronoun) is the indirect object in a sentence. It is also used after certain prepositions (see below right).

Although German has these four cases, people often avoid the genitive. For instance, to show whose something is, you often use *von* (of), followed by a dative noun, instead of the genitive (see page 12).

The two tables that follow show how the words for "the" and "a" change in the various cases. It is a good idea to learn these tables.

The words for "the"

	m	f	n	pl
nom	der	die	das	die
acc	den	die	das	die
gen	des	der	des	der
dat	dem	der	dem	den

The words for "a" or "an"

	m	f	n
nom	ein	eine	ein
acc	einen	eine	ein
gen	eines	einer	eines
dat	einem	einer	einem

The masculine, feminine, neuter and plural words for "this/that (thing)" ("these/those" in the plural) are *dieser, diese, dieses, diese*. These change like *der, die, das, die*, for example:

acc: *diesen, diese, dieses, diese*
dat: *diesem, dieser, diesem, diesen*

Words like *mein* (my), *dein* (your), *sein* (his, its), *ihr* (her, its), and so on (see page 50) change like *ein, eine, ein*. *Kein* (not a, not any, no – see page 54) also changes in the same way. The plural endings are shown below by the plural forms of *kein*:

nom & acc pl: *keine*
gen pl: *keiner*
dat pl: *keinen*

The nouns themselves (as opposed to the words that go with them) stay the same, except in a couple of instances. Here are the few changes you need to know:

1) In the dative plural, nouns add "n" (to their plural ending), except for those with a plural that ends in "s", which stay the same.

2) In the genitive singular, most masculine and neuter nouns add an "s". Short nouns (nouns of one syllable) that end in a consonant, and nouns that end in "s", "ß", "tz" or "sch", add "es".

Examples:
das Hotel (hotel) – genitive, *des Hotels* (or *eines Hotels*)
der Tag (day) – genitive, *des Tages* (or *eines Tages*)
das Schloß (castle) – genitive, *des Schlosses* (or *eines Schlosses*)

3) In the genitive, proper nouns (names) add "s", except for names that end in "s" or "z", which just add an apostrophe.

Prepositions

In German, prepositions (words like "in" and "from") used with a noun (or pronoun) always make the noun (or pronoun) go into a certain case. Most prepositions make the word change into the accusative or the dative case. A few prepositions take either case, depending on whether movement is involved. For a detailed explanation of this, and lists of prepositions, see page 22.

A few prepositions, for instance *wegen* (because of), are supposed to be followed by the genitive, but because this case is often avoided, the dative is sometimes used instead.

Prepositions followed by a word for "the" are often shortened. Those you will often hear or see written in everyday German are:

am (*an dem* – at/on the)
ans (*an das* – on (to) the)
aufs (*auf das* – on(to) the, up (to) the)
beim (*bei dem* – at/near the)
im (*in dem* – in the)
ins (*in das* – in(to) the)
zum (*zu dem* – to the)
zur (*zu der* – to the)

---

1 The "ß" on the end of *der Fluß* changes to "ss" in *die Flüsse*, which is what often happens when a vowel is added. Remember, "ß" and "ss" sound the same.

Adjectives

In German, adjectives used closely with a noun (as in "the small tent") change to match the noun's gender and go into the same case as the noun. Adjectives used with a noun but separated from it (e.g. by a verb) do not change. For example, with *klein* (small), you say *das kleine Zelt* (the small tent), but *Das Zelt ist klein* (The tent is small).

When an adjective has to change, there are three different patterns of change that it can follow. Each involves a set of endings being attached to the adjective. The pattern followed depends on whether the adjective is used after the words for "the" or "a" or alone with the noun. The tables below show the three patterns. The endings are shown attached to an adjective (*rot* – red), as this makes it easier to learn them.

Endings for adjectives used alone with the noun

	m	f	n	pl
nom	roter	rote	rotes	rote
acc	roten	rote	rotes	rote
gen	roten	roter	roten	roter
dat	rotem	roter	rotem	roten

Endings for adjectives used with the word for "the" and the noun

	m	f	n
nom	der rote	die rote	das rote
acc	den roten	die rote	das rote
gen	des roten	der roten	des roten
dat	dem roten	der roten	dem roten

	pl
nom	die roten
acc	die roten
gen	der roten
dat	den roten

Endings for adjectives used with the word for "a" and the noun

	m	f	n
nom	ein roter	eine rote	ein rotes
acc	einen roten	eine rote	ein rotes
gen	eines roten	einer roten	eines roten
dat	einem roten	einer roten	einem roten

When you use an adjective and a noun with certain words such as *dieser, diese, dieses, diese* (this) or *welcher, welche, welches, welche* (the question word "which"), the adjective takes the same endings as if you were using *der, die, das, die*. If you use an adjective and a noun with *kein* or with the words for "my", "your", "his", etc. (see above right), the adjective takes the same endings as if you were using *ein, eine, ein*, and the plural ending for the adjective is "en" in all four cases.

When you use the plural words *viele* (many) or *ein paar* (a few) with an adjective and a noun, the adjective takes the (plural) endings shown in the first table above.

Making comparisons

To make comparisons in German – to say, for example, "He's taller" or "She's more important", or "He's the tallest brother",

you use *-er* or *-(e)st* added on to the adjective. For a detailed explanation of comparisons, see page 44.

A few adjectives add an umlaut as well as the usual *-er* or *-(e)st* endings, for example *groß* (big, tall) becomes *größer* (bigger, taller) or *der/die/das größte* (the biggest, the tallest). The following list tells you which adjectives take this umlaut:

alt (old), *jung* (young), *lang* (long), *kurz* (short), *stark* (strong), *schwach* (weak), *klug* (clever, smart), *dumm* (stupid), *warm* (warm), *kalt* (cold), *groß* (big, tall), *arm* (poor), *hart* (hard), *scharf* (sharp), *krank* (ill), *hoch* (high), *nah* (near).[1]

"I", "you", "he", "she", etc. (*ich, du, er, sie*, etc.)

The German for "I" is *ich*.

The German for "you" is either *du, ihr* or *Sie*. For friends or relatives, you use *du* or *ihr* – *du* if you are talking to one person, and *ihr* if you are talking to more than one person.

Sie is the polite form. It is used for "you" when you are talking to anyone older or anyone you do not know well. This polite *Sie* is used in both the singular and the plural, so you use it for one person and for two or more people. It is always written with a capital "S".[2]

Whenever you are not sure whether you should use the familiar *du* or *ihr* or the polite *Sie*, use *Sie*. If the familiar form is all right, people will let you know. (There is a special verb, *duzen*, which means "to say *du*". Listen out for *Du kannst mich duzen*. It means "You can say *du* to me".) Usually, though, when a child or teenager talks to other children or teenagers, *du* and *ihr* are used.

The word for "he" is *er*, and the word for "she" is *sie*. To say "it", you use *er, sie* or *es* depending on the gender of the noun or pronoun you are referring to. You use *er* for anything masculine, *sie* for anything feminine and *es* for anything neuter. For example, talking about *der Rucksack* (rucksack), you say *Er ist blau* (It is blue), but for *die Tasche* (bag), you say *Sie ist blau* (It is blue), and for *das Gepäck* (luggage), you say *Es ist blau* (It is blue).

The German for "we" is *wir*.

The German for "they" is *sie*.

All these words (*ich, du* and so on) are called personal pronouns. This is because they stand in for the name of a person or thing. The forms shown above are those you use when the pronouns are the subject (as in "I am" or "they are singing"). They are in the nominative case.

There are other forms for when the pronouns are the direct or indirect object, for example in English, "I" becomes "me" ("I like dogs" but "Rover likes me" or "Rover gives me his lead"). In German, the pronouns have an accusative and dative case which you use in sentences like this,

and also after prepositions. You can see all their forms on page 28 (the genitive case is not shown as it is hardly ever used).

"My", "your", "his", "her", etc.

The basic words (the masculine singular nominative form) for "my", "your", etc. are shown below. They always agree with the noun they are used with and go into the same case. They take the same endings as *ein, eine, ein* in the singular and the same endings as *kein* in the plural (see page 49).

mein (my)	*unser* (our)
dein (your)	*euer*[3] (your)
sein (his/its)	*ihr* (their)
ihr (her/its)	*Ihr* (your)

As you can see, there are three words for "your". You use *dein* where you would say *du* for "you", *euer* where you would say *ihr*, and *Ihr* where you would say *Sie*. You always write *Ihr* (polite "your") with a capital "I".

"Mine", "yours", "his", "hers", etc.

There is a full table showing the German words for "mine", "yours", "his", "hers", etc. on page 38. These words change according to case like *der, die, das, die* (see page 49). For example, talking about a jumper (*der Pulli*), you say *Sie hat meinen* (She's got mine).

Verbs and the present tense

Verbs change to show when their action takes place. Tenses are the different forms that verbs adopt to do this. For example, "I/you/we/they take" and "he/she/it takes" are the present tense forms of "to take"; the past tense is "took".

In the present tense, most German verbs follow the regular pattern shown by *kochen* below. This means that to make the present tense, you take the verb's stem and add the endings *-e, -st, -t, -en, -t, -en, -en*. The stem is the infinitive (the basic form) minus "(e)n" (e.g. *koch-* is the stem of *kochen*).[4]

Kochen (to cook) – present tense

ich koche	I cook (am cooking)
du kochst	you cook
er/sie/es kocht	he/she/it cooks
wir kochen	we cook
ihr kocht	you cook
sie kochen	they cook
Sie kochen	you cook

Verbs with a stem ending in "d" or "t" add "est" and "et" instead of "st" and "t" in the *du* and *er* forms.

As you can see, the German present tense is used for an action that is happening now or one that happens regularly. This means that *ich koche* can either mean "I cook" or "I am/I'm cooking".

As in English, the present is also often used instead of the future tense for something that is going to happen in the future. For example, *Ich gehe am dritten August* is a

---

1 *Hoch* and *nah* change a bit more as well. You say *höher* (higher) and *der nächste* (the nearest). **2** In letters and cards, *du* and *ihr* also take a capital first letter, and so do the words for "your" and "yours". **3** In the plural, *euer* is usually written without its second "e". **4** The infinitive of most verbs ends in "en", and their stem is the infinitive minus "en". A few verbs end in a consonant + "n", e.g. *klettern*. For these, the stem is the infinitive minus "n".

present tense, meaning "I go on the 3rd of August", but it is actually about a future event. The future tense (see page 53) could be used, but the present is often preferred in both languages. In fact, German uses the present tense in this way even more often than English (for more about this, see the top of page 42).

Irregular verbs

Some of the most commonly used verbs are irregular. They do not form their present tense according to the regular pattern, so you have to learn how to form the present tense of each one.

There are three categories of irregular verbs:

1) A small number of special verbs, each of which is totally individual. They include the verbs *haben* (to have), *sein* (to be), *werden* (to become), *wissen* (to know) and *tun* (to do).

2) A set of six verbs called the modal verbs (see below).

3) A group of verbs that nearly follow the regular present tense pattern, but change a vowel in their stem in the *du* and *er* forms. For example, the present of *geben* (to give) is *ich gebe, du gibst, er/sie/es gibt, wir geben, ihr gebt, sie/Sie geben*. The vowel change may just be an added umlaut, (e.g. *du fährst, er fährt* from *fahren* – to go, to drive).

You can find the present tenses of all the verbs in categories **1)** and **2)** on pages 54-55, along with their other tense forms. The present tenses of the verbs in category **3)** are shown as part of the lists of strong verbs on page 52, where their other tense forms are also shown.

It is especially important to learn *haben, sein* and *werden*. Apart from being used a lot as verbs in their own right, these verbs are also used to form other tenses (see the perfect tense, pages 51-52, the future tense, page 53, and the conditional, page 53).

The modal verbs

The six modal verbs are *dürfen* (to be allowed to, may), *können* (to be able to, can), *mögen* (to like (to)), *müssen* (to have to, must) *sollen* (to be supposed to, should) and *wollen* (to want (to)). These verbs are used a lot, often with another verb in the infinitive, and this goes to the end of the sentence, for example *Ich muß den Brief finden* (I must find the letter). For a list of these verbs in their present (and other) tense forms, see page 55.

The imperfect tense (uses)

The imperfect tense is one of two main past tenses in German that you have to know. It is used for three types of past events:

a) For events that were in the process of happening at a particular point in the past – where English uses "was/were + (verb + ing)", as in "he was cycling" or "they were watching TV".

b) For an event that happened often in the past – where English can say "He cycled to school every day" or "He used to cycle to school".

c) For once-only events (e.g. where English says "That morning he cycled to school").

In practice, formal, written German generally keeps to these "rules" and uses the imperfect for all of these three types of past event. However, in everyday German you will find people using the perfect tense instead, particularly for once-only events (see next column), although they do mainly keep to the imperfect with certain very common verbs, such as *sein, haben* and the modal verbs.

Weak and strong verbs

In German, there are two main ways to form the imperfect tense, depending on whether the verb can be classified as weak or strong.

Weak verbs are those which use their present tense stem (the infinitive minus "(e)n") to form their imperfect tense, and other past tenses.

Strong verbs are those whose stems change in the imperfect tense (most also have a stem change in the other past tenses). Some are regular in the present tense, and others are irregular (they have a change in their stem in the *du* and *er* forms and make up category **3)** of the irregular present tense verbs – see left). You have to learn strong verbs as you come across them. The most useful ones are listed on page 52.

The irregular present tense verbs in category **1)**, above left, such as *sein*, have more or less unpredictable forms in the imperfect and other past tenses (except *wissen* – see Mixed verbs). You just have to learn them.[5] Their imperfect tenses are shown on pages 54-55. The way modal verbs (category **2)**) behave in the imperfect tense is explained above right.

To form the imperfect tense, weak verbs add one set of endings to their stem, and strong verbs add a different set of endings to their, different, imperfect stem. These two sets of endings are shown below and above right.

The imperfect of weak verbs

To form the imperfect of weak verbs, you take the verb's stem (the infinitive minus "(e)n") and add one of a set of imperfect endings. These are *-te, -test, -te, -ten, -tet, -ten, -ten*.[6] For example, here is he imperfect of *kochen*:

ich kochte	I was cooking (I cooked)
du kochtest	you were cooking
er/sie/es kochte	he/she/it was cooking
wir kochten	we were cooking
ihr kochtet	you were cooking
sie kochten	they were cooking
Sie kochten	you were cooking

Modal verbs form the imperfect in the same way as weak verbs, except that the four with an umlaut (*können, dürfen, mögen and müssen*) lose the umlaut, the "g" of *mögen* changes to "ch" and the "ss" of *müssen* becomes "ß" (see page 55).

The imperfect of strong verbs

To form the imperfect of strong verbs, you take their new, different stem (which you must learn – see page 52) and, in the *ich* and *er* forms, you add nothing. In the other forms, you add *-st, -en, -t, -en, -en* as shown by the imperfect of *singen* below:

ich sang	I was singing (sang)
du sangst	you were singing
er/sie/es sang	he/she/it was singing
wir sangen	we were singing
ihr sangt	you were singing
sie sangen	they were singing
Sie sangen	you were singing

Mixed verbs

German has a small number of mixed verbs. These have a special imperfect tense stem like strong verbs, but they take the weak verb endings. The four you need to know are *bringen* (to bring – imperfect stem: *brach-*), *denken* (to think – *dach-*), *kennen* (to know – *kann-*), all of which are regular in the present tense, and *wissen* (to know – imperfect stem: *wuß-*) which is irregular in the present tense.

The perfect tense (uses)

There are two main uses of the perfect tense[7] in German:

a) It is used where English uses "have/has" as in "I have read two of her books" or "She has travelled a lot".

b) It is used for once-only past events – events that happened just once at the time you are talking about or in the story you are telling. For example, in English, "That morning he cycled to school. He skidded on a banana skin and ended up in the pond".

The imperfect tense is meant to be used for this type of past event, but in practice this only happens in formal, written German (see top of previous column). In conversation and informal letters, everyone uses the perfect with just a few verbs in the imperfect mixed in. There is no rule about which verbs to use in which tense, but *sein, haben* and the modal verbs are more often used in the imperfect.

Forming the perfect tense

The German perfect tense is made of two bits. For most verbs, it is made from the present tense of *haben* (to have) and a special form of the verb you are using, called the past participle. For example, the past participle of *kochen* is *gekocht*, so the perfect tense *ich* form is *ich habe gekocht* (I have cooked, I cooked).

---

5 Category **1)** verbs are sometimes classed as strong verbs because they do not keep their present tense stem in the past tenses. However, they are exceptional verbs with unpredictable irregularities which must be learned in their various tenses, so it is best to treat them separately. **6** For verbs with a stem ending in "d" or "t", an extra "e" goes on the end of the stem, e.g. *ich arbeitete* (I worked, I was working) from *arbeiten* (to work). **7** The full name of this tense is the "present perfect".

For some verbs (see "Sein verbs" below), the perfect is made from the present tense of sein (to be) and the past participle. For example, the perfect tense ich form of klettern (to climb) is ich bin geklettert (I have climbed, I climbed).

In a sentence, the past participle always goes to the end, for example Ich habe etwas gekocht (I have cooked/cooked something).

Forming the past participle

The way the past participle is formed depends on whether the verb is weak or strong. For weak verbs, take the present tense stem (the infinitive minus "(e)n") and put "ge" on the front and "t" on the end. For kochen and klettern, for example, the past participles are gekocht and geklettert, as you have seen.

For strong verbs, the past participle also begins with "ge", but it ends with "en". You add these to a special perfect tense stem which you have to learn (see the box on the right). For some strong verbs, this stem is the same as the imperfect tense stem, for some it is the same as the present tense stem, and for others, it is a new stem. For example, the imperfect tense stem of schreiben (to write) is schrieb, and the past participle is geschrieben, whilst the imperfect stem of singen (to sing) is sang but its past participle is gesungen.[1]

To make the past participle of mixed verbs, use the imperfect stem and add "ge" at the start and "t" on the end, for example ich habe gedacht (I have thought, I thought).

For the irregular verbs in category 1) on page 51 (apart from wissen, which is a mixed verb), you have to learn the past participle (see pages 54-55).

"Sein verbs"

Most "sein verbs" (verbs using sein instead of haben to form the perfect tense) involve either a change of place (for example folgen – to follow) or of state (for example aufwachen – to wake up). There are a few sein verbs that do not involve a change like this, though, for example bleiben (to stay) and verbs that mean "to happen" (geschehen and passieren).

The verb werden and the verb sein itself are also sein verbs (see their perfect tenses on page 55).

Like the verbs that form the perfect tense with haben ("haben verbs"), some verbs that use sein to form their perfect tense are weak, others are strong (though most sein verbs are strong).

Weak sein verbs

Past participles are shown in brackets.

aufwachen (aufgewacht)	to wake up
begegnen (begegnet)	to meet, to bump into
folgen (gefolgt)	to follow
klettern (geklettert)	to climb
passieren (passiert)	to happen
stürzen (gestürzt)	to fall, to plunge

Strong verbs

The two lists below include most of the common strong verbs. They show you the parts you need to know to be able to form the various tenses. The present tense er form tells you whether the verb is irregular in the present; the imperfect er form gives you its imperfect stem; the perfect er form gives you the past participle and tells you if the verb is a haben or a sein verb. Try to learn these verbs.

Strong haben verbs

This list shows you the most useful strong verbs that form the perfect tense with haben.

infinitive	present	imperfect	perfect	
beginnen	beginnt	begann	hat begonnen	to begin, to start
bitten	bittet	bat	hat gebeten	to request, to ask
brechen	bricht	brach	hat gebrochen	to break
empfehlen	empfiehlt	empfahl	hat empfohlen	to recommend
essen	ißt	aß	hat gegessen	to eat
fangen	fängt	fing	hat gefangen	to catch
finden	findet	fand	hat gefunden	to find
geben	gibt	gab	hat gegeben	to give
genießen	genießt	genoß	hat genossen	to enjoy
greifen	greift	griff	hat gegriffen	to grab
halten	hält	hielt	hat gehalten	to stop, to hold
heißen	heißt	hieß	hat geheißen	to be called
helfen	hilft	half	hat geholfen	to help
lassen	läßt	ließ	hat gelassen	to let, to leave
leihen	leiht	lieh	hat geliehen	to lend
lesen	liest	las	hat gelesen	to read
nehmen	nimmt	nahm	hat genommen	to take
riechen	riecht	roch	hat gerochen	to smell
rufen	ruft	rief	hat gerufen	to call
scheinen	scheint	schien	hat geschienen	to shine, to seem
schieben	schiebt	schob	hat geschoben	to push, to shove
schlafen	schläft	schlief	hat geschlafen	to sleep
schlagen	schlägt	schlug	hat geschlagen	to hit, to strike
schließen	schließt	schloß	hat geschlossen	to shut
schneiden	schneidet	schnitt	hat geschnitten	to cut
schreiben	schreibt	schrieb	hat geschrieben	to write
sehen	sieht	sah	hat gesehen	to see
singen	singt	sang	hat gesungen	to sing
sprechen	spricht	sprach	hat gesprochen	to speak
stehen	steht	stand	hat gestanden	to stand
stehlen	stiehlt	stahl	hat gestohlen	to steal
tragen	trägt	trug	hat getragen	to carry
treffen	trifft	traf	hat getroffen	to meet
trinken	trinkt	trank	hat getrunken	to drink
vergessen	vergißt	vergaß	hat vergessen	to forget
verlieren	verliert	verlor	hat verloren	to lose
waschen	wäscht	wusch	hat gewaschen	to wash
werfen	wirft	warf	hat geworfen	to throw
zerreißen	zerreißt	zerriß	hat zerrissen	to tear into bits
ziehen	zieht	zog	hat gezogen	to pull

Strong sein verbs

This list shows you the most useful strong verbs that form the perfect tense with sein.

infinitive	present	imperfect	perfect	
bleiben	bleibt	blieb	ist geblieben	to stay
fahren	fährt	fuhr	ist gefahren	to go, to drive
fallen	fällt	fiel	ist gefallen	to fall
fliegen	fliegt	flog	ist geflogen	to fly
gehen	geht	ging	ist gegangen	to go, to walk
geschehen	geschieht	geschah	ist geschehen	to happen
kommen	kommt	kam	ist gekommen	to come
laufen	läuft	lief	ist gelaufen	to run
schwimmen	schwimmt	schwamm	ist geschwommen	to swim
springen	springt	sprang	ist gesprungen	to jump
steigen	steigt	stieg	ist gestiegen	to climb
sterben	stirbt	starb	ist gestorben	to die
wachsen	wächst	wuchs	ist gewachsen	to grow

---

52   [1] There a few verbs (some weak, some strong) that do not add "ge": verbs ending in "ieren", verbs that already begin with "ge" and verbs that begin with an inseparable prefix (e.g. be-, er-, ver-; see page 53). For separable verbs (see page 53), the "ge" goes in after the separable prefix, e.g. for aufwachen (to wake up), the past participle is aufgewacht.

The future tense

To talk about the future – where, in English, you would either say "I will/I'll cook" or "I am/I'm going to cook", German often just uses the present tense (this is fully explained on page 42). However, German has a future tense which it also uses.

The future tense is very easy to form. For all verbs, it is made from the present tense of *werden* (to become) + the infinitive of the verb you are using. For example, here is the future tense of *kochen*:

ich werde kochen	I will cook
du wirst kochen	you will cook
er/sie/es wird kochen	he/she/it will cook
wir werden kochen	we will cook
ihr werdet kochen	you will cook
sie werden kochen	they will cook
Sie werden kochen	you will cook

The imperative

The imperative form of a verb is used when you want to give a command – where, in English, for example, you say "Come here!". Clearly, commands like this are always addressed to "you" (rather than "he", "she" and so on).

To make the imperative of most verbs, you take the present tense *du*, *ihr* or *Sie* form, depending on the word you are using for "you". For the *du* form, you drop the word *du* and the "st" ending on the verb. For the *ihr* form you just drop *ihr*. For the *Sie* form, you keep *Sie* but move it after the verb.

Examples:
Warte! (Wait!)
Wartet! (Wait!)
Warten Sie! (Wait!)

This rule applies to almost all verbs. Whether they are regular or irregular in the present tense, their present tense "you" forms are used to form the imperative. The only exceptions are *sein*, *werden* and *wissen*, which have irregular imperatives (see page 55), modal verbs, which are not used in the imperative, and those irregular present tense verbs in category **3)** on page 51 which add an umlaut in the *du* (and *er*) form. This umlaut is dropped from the imperative *du* form.

The conditional

In German, the conditional form (the "would" form, as in "I would buy it now, but I haven't got any money") is made from a form of *werden* (shown below) + the infinitive of the verb you are using. For example, here is the conditional form of *kochen*:

ich würde kochen	I would/I'd cook
du würdest kochen	you would cook
er/sie/es würde kochen	he/she/it would cook
wir würden kochen	we would cook
ihr würdet kochen	you would cook
sie würden kochen	they would cook
Sie würden kochen	you would cook

For *sein*, *haben* and the modal verbs, you can use the conditional in this way (e.g. *ich würde haben*), but you more often use another, shorter method. For *haben* and the modal verbs, this is formed by taking the imperfect tense form (see pages 54-55), and adding an umlaut to all but *sollen* and *wollen*. The *ich* forms, for example, are as follows:

ich hätte	I would have
ich dürfte	I would be allowed to
ich könnte·	I would be able to, I could
ich möchte	I would like (to)
ich müßte	I would have to
ich sollte	I should, I ought to
ich wollte	I would want (to)

For *sein*, this alternative "would" form follows the above rule but also adds an "e" in some forms. It is shown below:

ich wäre (I would be), *du wär(e)st, er/sie/es wäre, wir wären, ihr wär(e)t, sie wären, Sie wären.*[2]

Reflexive verbs

Reflexive verbs are verbs such as *sich waschen* (to have a wash) that are used with the words *mich, dich, sich, uns* and *euch*. Their infinitive form always begins with the word *sich* (see the present tense of *sich waschen* below).

These verbs imply an action that you do to yourself. Indeed the words listed above translate as "myself" (*mich*), "yourself" (*dich*), and so on. However, you do not normally use "myself", "yourself", etc. in the English translations, as there are other ways to translate the verbs that sound more natural in English.

Sich waschen (to have a wash)

ich wasche mich	I have (am having) a wash
du wäschst dich	you have a wash
er/sie/es wäscht sich	he/she/it has a wash
wir waschen uns	we have a wash
ihr wascht euch	you have a wash
sie waschen sich	they have a wash
Sie waschen sich	you have a wash

Reflexive verbs can be weak or strong. They all form the perfect tense with *haben*. In the perfect, the words *mich, dich, sich*, and so on, go after the *haben* part of the verb, for example *Ich habe mich heute früh gewaschen* (I had a wash this morning).

The imperative (see above left) is made in just the same way as for other verbs. You keep the words *dich, euch* and *sich*, as they are part of the *du, ihr* and *Sie* forms. For example, with *sich setzen* (to sit down), you say:

Setz dich (Sit down)
Setzt euch (Sit down)
Setzen Sie sich (Sit down)

As you can see, the reflexive words, *mich, dich, sich, uns, euch* and *sich*, are similar to the accusative personal pronouns (see page 28). This is because they are thought of as the direct object of the reflexive verb (literally, *ich wasche mich* means "I wash myself").

Sometimes, though, you use another set of reflexive pronouns. These are *mir, dir, sich, uns, euch* and *sich*. They are in the dative case and are similar to the dative personal pronouns (see page 28). You use these when another direct object, such as "hands" or "face" is involved. German then treats "myself", "yourself" and so on as indirect objects, which is why they go into the dative. For example, *Ich wasche mir die Hände* means literally "I wash to myself the hands", though English just says "I wash my hands".

Separable verbs

Separable verbs are verbs which, in the infinitive, are made of two parts: a basic verb (which can be weak or strong) + an extra word joined to the front. The extra word is called a prefix. For example, *zumachen* (to close) is made up of *machen* (to make, to do) and the prefix *zu*.

When you use separable verbs in the various tenses and forms (except the perfect tense), the prefix separates off and goes to the end of the sentence, for example *Er macht die Tür zu* (He closes the door). In the perfect, the "ge" slots in between the prefix and the verb proper, and the prefix stays at the beginning, for example *Er hat die Tür zugemacht* (He closed/has closed the door). In the imperative, the prefix goes at the end, e.g. *Mach die Tür zu, Macht die Tür zu, Machen Sie die Tür zu* (Close the door).

By learning the following list of common prefixes, you will be able to spot separable verbs:[3]

ab, an, auf, aus, da, dahin, dorthin, durch, ein, her, herein, herum, hierher, hin, hinein, hinunter, los, mit, nach, vor, weg, weiter, um, zu, zurück, zusammen.

If you compare these with the prepositions on page 22, you will notice that many prefixes can also be prepositions, and, as such, words in their own right. In fact, with experience, you will learn that prefixes have a rough meaning which is often similar to that of the related prepositions. This can help to work out what a particular separable verb means (e.g. *aufessen* means "to eat up" from *auf* – up, and *essen* – to eat).

Inseparable prefixes

German has a few inseparable prefixes. These are *be-, emp-, ent-, er-, ge-, miß-, ver-* and *zer-*.[4] These prefixes are at the beginning of certain verbs, and they always remain there, for example, from *verlieren* (to lose): *ich verliere* (I am losing).

Negative sentences – *nicht* and *kein*

Nicht The German for "not" is *nicht*. If you use *nicht* in a sentence that has a direct or an indirect object (or both), *nicht* comes after the object(s), for example:

Ich habe den Schlüssel nicht (I have not/haven't got the key)
Er gab es mir nicht (He did not/didn't give it to me)

---

2 The "e"s shown in brackets are often dropped in spoken German. **3** The word list on pages 59-64 shows separable verbs with a / between the prefix and the basic verb (e.g. *auf/essen* – to eat up). **4** Watch out for the prefix *be-*. It must be pronounced separately from the rest of the verb, even if this verb starts with a vowel. For example, *beeilen* is said "ba-eylen".

If you use *nicht* in a sentence with no object(s), it normally follows the verb, for example:

Ich rauche nicht (I don't smoke)
Sie ist nicht dumm (She's not stupid)

When *nicht* is used in a sentence with two verbs or with a verb in two bits (e.g. a verb in the perfect or future tense, or a separable verb), it goes before the second verb or second bit, for example:

Ich will nicht tanzen (I don't want to dance)
Ich habe es nicht gesehen (I haven't seen it)
Er macht die Tür nicht zu (He does not close the door)

Kein You do not say *nicht ein* in German. Instead, wherever you would need to put *nicht* before *ein, eine, ein* (a, an), you use *kein, keine, kein* (not a/an, not any, no). These change in exactly the same way as *ein, eine, ein* in the various cases (see page 49). *Keine*, the plural, means "not any" or "no" when you are talking about more than one thing (its plural case endings are also on page 49).

Examples:
Das ist keine Katze (That's not a cat)
Ich habe keinen Schlüssel (I haven't got a key, I have no key)
Wir haben keine Bonbons (We haven't got any sweets, We've got no sweets)

Making questions

To make questions in German, you simply put the subject after the verb, for example:

Hast du meinen Pulli? (Do you have/Have you got my jumper?)
Wo wohnen Sie? (Where do you live?)

The most useful question words (words like *wo?* – where?, or *warum?* – why?) are listed on page 16.

German word order summary

In German, words are not always used in the same order as in English. Here is a summary of the differences you have to know about.

1) In English, the normal word order is subject, verb, object (e.g. "He drinks tea"). If you add some detail, this detail can go at the start or the end ("He drinks tea for breakfast" or "For breakfast, he drinks tea"), but you keep the same basic order (subject, verb, object).

In German, the usual word order is the same (e.g. *Er trinkt Tee* – He drinks tea). However, as in English, you may choose to put some detail first. If you do, the word order changes. The verb must come next (after the detail), followed by the subject. The detail could be just one word (e.g. *dann* – then, or *später* – later), or could be far longer (e.g. a whole clause – see **2)** in the next column).

Examples:
Zum Frühstück trinkt er Tee (For breakfast, he drinks tea)
In Berlin fand ich ein gutes Hotel (I found a good hotel in Berlin)
Dann sah ich ihn (Then I saw him)

Although in German you do not have to put the detail first, this is more common than in English, especially with words for time (e.g. "then", "later" and so on).

In English a sentence can start with the direct object (e.g. "That I didn't know"), though it does not happen often. In German it happens a lot, sometimes for emphasis, but often just as a matter of style, especially with a short direct object. When it happens, you must again put the verb in second position with the subject after it, for example *Tee trinkt er gern* (He likes tea) and *Das wußte ich nicht* (I didn't know that).

2) In German, when you have a long sentence with a main clause and another clause,[1] called a subordinate clause (which often begins with a word like "because", "who", "which" or "that"), a comma separates them and the verb in the subordinate clause goes to the end.

Examples:
Ich bleibe hier, weil ich müde bin
OR
Weil ich müde bin, bleibe ich hier (I'm staying here because I'm tired).

Notice how, if the subordinate clause is first (as in the second example above), it plays the part of detail placed before the main verb, so the rule given in **1)** applies (the main verb is in second position, after the detail, with the subject after it).

For more about using *weil* (because), see page 26. For more about the German for "who", "which" or "that", see page 24.

3) In a main clause or a simple, one-clause sentence, if you have a verb made of two bits, such as a verb in the perfect or future tenses, or one in the conditional, the second bit goes to the end of the clause, for example:

Ich habe einen schweren Rucksack getragen (I've carried/I carried a heavy rucksack)

However, if you use a verb in two bits in a subordinate clause, the rule about the verb having to go to the end of the clause applies (see **2)** above), and the first bit goes to the end with the second bit just before it, for example:

Ich bin müde, weil ich einen schweren Rucksack getragen habe (I'm tired because I've carried a heavy rucksack)

The same thing happens when you use a modal verb with an infinitive verb. In a main clause or short sentence, the infinitive must go to the end (*Ich muß seinen Rucksack tragen* – I have to carry his rucksack). In a subordinate clause, the modal verb goes to the end with the

infinitive just before it (*Ich bin müde, weil ich seinen Rucksack tragen muß* – I'm tired because I have to carry his rucksack).

4) Some little words do not have any effect on the word order. These include *ja* (yes), *nein* (no), *na gut* (right) and *also* (right, so). You can put them at the start of the sentence (usually with a comma) and the rest of the sentence carries on as if they were not there. For example, *Ja, er trinkt Tee* (Yes, he drinks tea).

When you listen to German speakers, you will also notice a few little words such as *bloß, denn, doch, mal, schon* and so on. These words improve the flow or rhythm of the sentence, but they often do not really mean much (and are not always translated). *Ja* is also used in this way, normally to reinforce what you are saying. With practice you will learn to spot when it is natural to use these little words.

Examples:
Ja, ich glaube schon (Yes, I think so)
Ich muß ihm schon mal schreiben (I (really) must write to him)
Was machen wir denn? (What shall we do (then)?)

Irregular and modal verbs

For the special, irregular verbs in category **1)**, page 51 (*haben, sein, werden, wissen* and *tun*) and the modal verbs (category **2)**, page 51), it is best to learn the tenses individually.

These verbs are shown here in the tenses and forms you will need. For each, the present and imperfect tenses are given, as well as the perfect tense *er* form (which shows you the verb's past participle and whether it is a *haben* or *sein* verb).

Remember, to make the future tense, take the present tense of *werden* with the infinitive of the verb you are using (e.g. *ich werde wissen* – I will know).

Haben (to have, to have got)

present tense
ich habe	I have (got)
du hast	you have (got)
er/sie/es hat	he/she/it has (got)
wir haben	we have (got)
ihr habt	you have (got)
sie haben	they have (got)
Sie haben	you have (got)

imperfect tense
ich hatte	I had (got)
du hattest	you had (got)
er/sie/es hatte	he/she/it had (got)
wir hatten	we had (got)
ihr hattet	you had (got)
sie hatten	they had (got)
Sie hatten	you had (got)

perfect tense (er form): *hat gehabt* (has had)

imperative: *hab(e),*[2] *habt, haben Sie* (have)

1 "Clause" and "main clause" are explained on page 5. 2 The "e" is often dropped.

Sein (to be)

present tense

ich bin	I am
du bist	you are
er/sie/es ist	he/she/it is
wir sind	we are
ihr seid	you are
sie sind	they are
Sie sind	you are

imperfect tense

ich war	I was
du warst	you were
er/sie/es war	he/she/it was
wir waren	we were
ihr wart	you were
sie waren	they were
Sie waren	you were

perfect tense (er form): *ist gewesen* (has been)

imperative: *sei, seid, seien Sie* (be)

Werden (to become)

present tense

ich werde	I become
du wirst	you become
er/sie/es wird	he/she/it becomes
wir werden	we become
ihr werdet	you become
sie werden	they become
Sie werden	you become

imperfect tense

ich wurde	I became
du wurdest	you became
er/sie/es wurde	he/she/it became
wir wurden	we became
ihr wurdet	you became
sie wurden	they became
Sie wurden	you became

perfect tense (er form): *ist geworden* (has become)

imperative: *werde, werdet, werden Sie* (become)

Wissen (to know)

present tense

ich weiß	I know
du weißt	you know
er/sie/es weiß	he/she/it knows
wir wissen	we know
ihr wißt	you know
sie wissen	they know
Sie wissen	you know

imperfect tense

ich wußte	I knew
du wußtest	you knew
er/sie/es wußte	he/she/it knew
wir wußten	we knew
ihr wußtet	you knew
sie wußten	they knew
Sie wußten	you knew

perfect tense (er form): *hat gewußt* (has known)

imperative: (rarely used) *wisse, wisset* (or *wißt*), *wissen Sie* (know)

Tun (to do)

present tense

ich tu(e)[2]	I do (am doing)
du tust	you do
er/sie/es tut	he/she/it does
wir tun	we do
ihr tut	you do
sie tun	they do
Sie tun	you do

imperfect tense

ich tat	I did
du tatest	you did
er/sie/es tat	he/she/it did
wir taten	we did
ihr tatet	you did
sie taten	they did
Sie taten	you did

perfect tense (er form): *hat getan* (has done)

imperative: *tu(e), tut, tun Sie* (do)

Modal verbs

Dürfen (to be allowed to, may)

present tense

ich darf	I may
du darfst	you may
er/sie/es darf	he/she/it may
wir dürfen	we may
ihr durft	you may
sie dürfen	they may
Sie dürfen	you may

imperfect tense

ich durfte	I was allowed to
du durftest	you were allowed to
er/sie/es durfte	he/she/it was allowed to
wir durften	we were allowed to
ihr durftet	you were allowed to
sie durften	they were allowed to
Sie durften	you were allowed to

perfect tense (er form): *hat gedurft* (has been allowed to)

Können (to be able to, can)

present tense

ich kann	I can
du kannst	you can
er/sie/es kann	he/she/it can
wir können	we can
ihr könnt	you can
sie können	they can
Sie können	you can

imperfect tense

ich konnte	I could (was able to)
du konntest	you could
er/sie/es konnte	he/she/it could
wir konnten	we could
ihr konntet	you could
sie konnten	they could
Sie konnten	you could

perfect tense (er form): *hat gekonnt* (has been able to)

Mögen (to like)

present tense

ich mag	I like
du magst	you like
er/sie/es mag	he/she/it likes
wir mögen	we like
ihr mögt	you like
sie mögen	they like
Sie mögen	you like

imperfect tense

ich mochte	I liked
du mochtest	you liked
er/sie/es mochte	he/she/it liked
wir mochten	we liked
ihr mochtet	you liked
sie mochten	they liked
Sie mochten	you liked

perfect tense (er form): *hat gemocht* (has liked)

Müssen (to have to, must)

present tense

ich muß	I must
du mußt	you must
er/sie/es muß	he/she/it must
wir müssen	we must
ihr müßt	you must
sie müssen	they must
Sie müssen	you must

imperfect tense

ich mußte	I had to
du mußtest	you had to
er/sie/es mußte	he/she/it had to
wir mußten	we had to
ihr mußtet	you had to
sie mußten	they had to
Sie mußten	you had to

perfect tense (er form): *hat gemußt* (has had to)

Sollen (should, to be supposed to)

present tense

ich soll	I am supposed to
du sollst	you are supposed to
er/sie/es soll	he/she/it is supposed to
wir sollen	we are supposed to
ihr sollt	you are supposed to
sie sollen	they are supposed to
Sie sollen	you are supposed to

imperfect tense

ich sollte	I was supposed to
du solltest	you were supposed to
er/sie/es sollte	he/she/it was supposed to
wir sollten	we were supposed to
ihr solltet	you were supposed to
sie sollten	they were supposed to
Sie sollten	you were supposed to

perfect tense (er form): *hat gesollt* (has been supposed to)

Wollen (to want to)

present tense

ich will	I want to
du willst	you want to
er/sie/es will	he/she/it wants to
wir wollen	we want to
ihr wollt	you want to
sie wollen	they want to
Sie wollen	you want to

imperfect tense

ich wollte	I wanted to
du wolltest	you wanted to
er/sie/es wollte	he/she/it wanted to
wir wollten	we wanted to
ihr wolltet	you wanted to
sie wollten	they wanted to
Sie wollten	you wanted to

perfect tense (er form): *hat gewollt* (has wanted to)

Answers to quizzes and puzzles

Page 7 Getting to the Blumenkohl house

ein Café   *ein Bauernhof*
ein Dorf   *eine Brücke*
ein See

Page 9 What is their luggage like?

2 *Ihr Gepäck ist grau.*
3 *Seine Tasche ist blau.*
4 *Ihr Koffer ist grün.*
5 *Seine Aktentasche ist rot.*
6 *Ihr Rucksack ist gelb.*

Page 11 The mysterious letter

Eine verlassene Insel, 1893

Mein lieber Sohn Georg,

   *Ich bin ein **alter** Mann. Ich bin hier ganz allein, und mein **Haus** in der Nähe von Turmstadt steht leer. Ich habe ein Geheimnis. Ich bin sehr reich. Du **bekommst** jetzt **meinen ganzen** Schatz. Du **findest den ersten** Hinweis in Blumenkohl-Haus. Du suchst die zwei Schiffe.*

Leb wohl, Tobias Blumenkohl

A desert island, 1893

My dear son George,

   I am an old man, I am all alone here, and my house near Turmstadt stands empty. I have a secret. I am very wealthy. You now get all my treasure. You can find the first clue in Blumenkohl house. You're looking for the two ships.

Farewell, Tobias Blumenkohl

Page 13 *Wem gehört das?*

2 *Dieser Tisch gehört den Nachbarn.*
3 *Diese Jacke gehört dem Untermieter.*
4 *Dieses Hemd gehört Heidrun.*
5 *Dieses Jeans gehören Erich* OR *Diese Hose gehört Erich.*
6 *Diese Werkzeuge gehören dem Handwerker.*

Page 15 The way to the old church

Geht nach links.
Geht über die Brücke.
Nehmt den zweiten Weg links und
geht (immer) geradeaus.
Geht nach rechts/Nehmt den ersten Weg nach rechts.

Page 17 Shopping quiz

Ich möchte ein Eis.
Wieviel/Was kosten sie?
Was für (ein) Kuchen ist das? OR *Was für eine Torte ist das?*
Ich möchte ein Kilo Äpfel OR *Kann ich ein Kilo Äpfel haben?*
Wo ist der Supermarkt?
Können Sie meinen Korb tragen?

What does the letter mean?

Er ist Monikas Urgroßvater OR *Er ist der Urgroßvater von Monika.*
Die zwei Schiffe/Sie sind Bilder.
Monika, Erich und Tanja/Sie müssen das Atelier anschauen OR *Sie müssen Heidruns Atelier anschauen* OR *Sie müssen das Atelier von Heidrun/von Monikas Mutter anschauen.*

Page 19 The first clue

Es gibt keine Würfel. [pl]
Es gibt keine Kerze. [f sing]
Es gibt keinen Vogel. [m sing]
Es gibt kein Buch. [n sing]
Es gibt keinen Zylinder. [m sing]

They have to go to Der Zauberer (The Magician Inn).

Page 21 Crossword puzzle

Across
1 *essen*
5 *sie*
6 *nimm*
8 *trägt*
9 *ab*
10 *hau*
11 *gern*

Down
2 *siehst du*
2 *nie*
4 *es gibt*
5 *spricht*
7 *fängt*
9 *an*

Page 23 The clue from the inn

(Sie/die Kuh steht) auf dem Hügel.
(Er/der Hund steht) unter dem Baum (OR neben dem Baum OR beim Baum).
(Sie/die Bank ist) dem Brunnen gegenüber (OR vor dem Brunnen Or beim Brunnen).
(Er/der Bauernhof ist) neben der Kirche.

Tanja's sentence ends:
. . .zur schule.

Page 25 A postcard from Tanja

Die Nachbarn (von Monikas Eltern/ der Eltern von Monika) haben eine Ziege.
Dieter/Er ist der Untermieter (von Monikas Eltern/der Eltern von Monika).
Tanja und Erich/Sie dürfen die alten Fahrräder benutzen.
Erich/Er wacht um acht Uhr (morgens) auf.
Erich und Tanja/Sie essen und waschen sich im Haus.
Die kleine Stadt, die Tanja gefällt,/ Sie heißt Alterhaven.

Page 27 Mix and match

Wir können nicht kommen, weil wir gerade essen.
Ich nehme dein Fahrrad, um nach Alterhaven zu fahren.
Wir kennen Frau Salbe, weil sie in der Apotheke arbeitet.
Sei ruhig! Ich denke gerade nach, weil es sehr schwierig ist.
Sie fährt nach Turmstadt, um einzukaufen.
Der Mechaniker ist da, weil die Maschine kaputt ist.

Page 29 the postcard jigsaw

Herrn Stefan Speck
Bahnhofstr. 3
1000 Berlin

Lieber Stefan,
Vielen Dank für Deinen Brief. Ja, Lothar und Anna Lauterback wohnen in der Nähe von Turmstadt. Du bittest mich um ihre Adresse. Hier ist sie: Dreieich Bauernhof, Brückenstraße, bei Alterhaven. Aber warum Turmstadt? Turmstadt ist nicht sehr interessant. Jedenfalls, sie haben wahrscheinlich ein Zimmer frei für Dich. Ich empfehle sie Dir. Bei ihnen ißt man gut und es ist dort schön ruhig. Also, schöne Ferien!

Natascha

Mr Stefan Speck
3 Bahnhofstraße
1000 Berlin

Dear Stefan,
Many thanks for your letter. Yes, Lothar and Anna Lauterback live near Turmstadt. You ask me for their address. Here it is: Dreieich Farm,

Brückenstraße, near Alterhaven. But why Turmstadt? Turmstadt's not very interesting. Anyhow they probably have a room for you. I recommend them to you. You eat well at their place and it's lovely and quiet there. So, have a nice holiday!

Natascha

Page 31 Picture puzzle

1c 2d 3b 4f 5e 6a

Page 33 Tobias Blumenkohl's disappearance

Rarafugalstadt

Dear Sir,
Unfortunately, your father is probably dead. He knew our islands well but at the time of his disappearance he was looking for plants on dangerous remote islands. He was working together with two fellow botanists. They had a good boat, but it was the stormy season.

Pedro Peperoni
Governor of the Rarafugal Islands

Page 35 Using past tenses

Zwei Freunde, Freddi und Ali, wollten Jeans kaufen und gingen in die Stadt. Später erzählte Freddi seiner Mutter davon: "Ich habe Ali in der Stadt getroffen. Wir haben überall gute Jeans gesucht. In einem Geschäft haben wir zwei Schlüssel in einer Hosentasche gefunden und wir haben sie dem Inhaber gegeben. Er sagte: "Die Schlüssel zu meinem Geldschrank! Danke schön! Gestern habe ich sie verloren. Ich habe sie überall gesucht, aber ich konnte sie nicht finden." Und dann hat er uns die Jeans umsonst gegeben! Wir haben heute Glück gehabt!"

Page 37 Say it in German

Herr Speck hat den alten Turm gesucht, aber er hat ihn nicht gefunden.
Tanja, Erich und Monika sind zum Bauernhof gegangen.
Sie haben ihn gefunden.
Herr Speck hat sie nicht gesehen.
Tanja und Monika haben sich unter dem Fenster versteckt.

Page 39 The writing on the tower

We have kept this old tower as a monument for the inhabitants of Turmstadt.
The pirates of Pirate Island destroyed it three years ago but now we have got our revenge. We have won our last battle against them. We have driven them out of their fort on the island and they have disappeared from our country.

Page 41 The false trail

Mein lieber Sohn, nun hast Du alle Hinweise, die ich hinterlassen habe, gefunden. Hier ist Deine letzte Aufgabe. Sie wird schwierig sein. Du wirst zur Polizeiwache in Alterhaven gehen müssen. Dort wirst Du ein Fenster ohne Gitter sehen. Auf diese Weise wirst Du hineingehen. Drinnen wirst Du eine mit Holzplatten verkleidete Wand sehen. Dort wirst Du alle meine Juwelen und mein Vermögen finden. Leb wohl, T.B.

My dear son, Now you have found all the clues I left behind. Here is your last task. It will be difficult. You will have to go to the police station in Alterhaven. There you will see one window without bars. You will go in that way. Inside you will see a wall with wooden panels. There you will find all my jewels and my fortune.
Farewell, T.B.

Page 43 Talking about the future

Susanne wird hier sein.
Ich hol's OR Ich hole ihn/sie/es.
Heute abend gehen wir ins Kino OR Wir gehen heute abend ins Kino.
Wirst du mir schreiben?
Richard kommt bald nach Hause.
Morgen schreibe ich den Brief OR Ich schreibe morgen den Brief.
Sie werden einen Kuchen/eine Torte mitbringen OR Sie werden einen Kuchen/eine Torte bringen.

Page 45 Which is the longest tunnel?

Der längste Tunnel ist Monikas (Tunnel) OR Der längste Tunnel ist der Tunnel von Monika.

Page 47 What if?

Ich würde alles ausgeben.
Ich würde das Dach reparieren lassen.
Du würdest ein neues Fahrrad bekommen.
Wir würden nach Amerika fahren, um meine Tante zu besuchen.

Page 48 Monika's letter

Monday 2 September
Dear Tanja and Erich,
Here is the article from the Messenger which tells our story. It's brilliant! What are you doing with your share of the reward? I'm going to buy myself a cassette recorder with mine. If your mother agrees, I'll visit you during the Christmas holidays. So, see you soon I hope!
Love from Monika

The newspaper article

The Blumenkohl family treasure.

Monika Blumenkohl with her friends Erich and Tanja Müller and her dog, Hüpfer.

Stefan Speck, the rare bird thief, who wanted to steal the Blumenkohl treasure.

The month of August has been an exciting time for Monika Blumenkohl and her friends Erich and Tanja. They found some treasure and helped the police catch the criminal Stefan Speck.

Many years ago, Monika's great-grandfather, Tobias, died on a remote island. He left behind a chest. This chest was hidden next to the entrance to a cave. A few months ago, Speck was on this same island. He was looking for some very rare parrots there that he wanted to steal.

By chance, he came across the old chest and found a letter from Tobias in it. This letter was addressed to Monika's grandfather, Georg. It was the first clue in a treasure hunt and brought Speck to Turmstadt, where he stupidly lost it. Erich and Tanja, who were just arriving to spend a few days with their friend Monika, found it. The three young people managed to find the treasure (gold), which was hidden in the old Pirates' Fort, before the criminal could do so. They also helped the police catch Speck. The three heroes also received a reward of 5,000 marks from the police. Our congratulations to them!

Numbers and other useful words

Here you will find some useful lists of words and expressions. Remember that telling the time is explained on page 24 and directions are on page 15.

Essential expressions

guten Tag	hello
(auf) Wiedersehen	goodbye
(auf) Wiederhören	goodbye (on telephone)
hallo	hi
tschüs	bye
guten Morgen	good morning
guten Abend	good evening, good night
gute Nacht	good night
bis bald	see you soon
bis nachher	see you later
ja	yes
nein	no
vielleicht	maybe
bitte	please
danke (schön)	thank you (very much)
entschuldige, entschuldigt, entschuldigen Sie, Entschuldigung	excuse me
es tut mir leid, Entschuldigung	I'm sorry
bitte schön	you're welcome
Ich verstehe nicht.	I don't understand.
Ich weiß nicht.	I don't know.
Was bedeutet dieses Wort?	What does this word mean?
Wie sagt man das auf Deutsch?	What's the German for this?

Numbers

0	null	17	siebzehn
1	eins	18	achtzehn
2	zwei	19	neunzehn
3	drei	20	zwanzig
4	vier	21	einundzwanzig
5	fünf	22	zweiundzwanzig
6	sechs	23	dreiundzwanzig
7	sieben	30	dreißig
8	acht	31	einunddreißig
9	neun	32	zweiunddreißig
10	zehn	40	vierzig
11	elf	50	fünfzig
12	zwölf	60	sechzig
13	dreizehn	70	siebzig
14	vierzehn	80	achtzig
15	fünfzehn	90	neunzig
16	sechzehn		

100 einhundert (one hundred), hundert (a hundred)
101 hunderteins

150	hundertfünfzig
200	zweihundert
300	dreihundert
1 000	tausend
1 100	tausendeinhundert, elfhundert
2 000	zweitausend
10 000	zehntausend
100 000	hunderttausend
1 000 000	eine Million
2 000 000	zwei Millionen
1 000 000 000	eine Milliarde

"The first", "second", "third", etc.

The German for "the first" is der/die/das erste. For other numbers up to nineteen, you add -te to the number (except for drei, sieben and acht – see below). For numbers twenty and over, you add -ste:

der/die/das erste	the first
der/die/das zweite	the second
der/die/das dritte	the third
der/die/das siebte	the seventh
der/die/das achte	the eighth
der/die/das zwanzigste	the twentieth
der/die/das einunddreißigste	the thirty first

Months, seasons and days

der Januar	January
der Februar	February
der März	March
der April	April
der Mai	May
der Juni	June
der Juli	July
der August	August
der September	September
der Oktober	October
der November	November
der Dezember	December
der Frühling	spring
der Sommer	summer
der Herbst	autumn
der Winter	winter
der Montag	Monday
der Dienstag	Tuesday
der Mittwoch	Wednesday
der Donnerstag	Thursday
der Freitag	Friday
der Samstag	Saturday
der Sonntag	Sunday
der Monat(-e)	month
die Jahreszeit(en)	season
das Jahr(e)	year
der Tag(e)	day
die Woche(n)	week

das Wochenende(n)	week-end
gestern	yesterday
heute	today
morgen	tomorrow
vorgestern	the day before yesterday
übermorgen	the day after tomorrow
diese Woche	this week
letzte Woche	last week
heute nachmittag	this afternoon
heute abend	this evening, tonight

Dates

das Tagebuch(¨er)	diary
der Kalender(-)	calendar
Den wievielten haben wir heute?	What's the date today?
am Montag	on Monday
im August	in August
am ersten April	on the first of April
am dritten März	on the third of March

1992 neunzehnhundertzweiundneunzig
1993 neunzehnhundertdreiundneunzig
1999 neunzehnhundertneunundneunzig
2000 zweitausend

Weather

das Wetter	weather
das Klima(s)	climate
die Wettervorhersage(n)	weather forecast
die Temperatur(en)	temperature
der Grad(e)	degree
Wie hoch steht das Thermometer?	What's the temperature?
Wie ist das Wetter?	What's the weather like?
Das Wetter ist schön, Es ist schön.	It's fine.
Das Wetter/Es ist schlecht.	The weather's bad, It's bad weather.
Es regnet.	It's raining.
Es ist heiß.	It's hot.
Es ist sonnig.	It's sunny.
Die Sonne scheint.	The sun's shining.
Es ist kalt.	It's cold.
Es schneit.	It's snowing.
der Himmel	sky
die Sonne	sun
der Regen	rain
die Wolke(n)	cloud
der Frost	frost
der Schnee	snow
der Hagel	hail

German-English word list

This list contains all the German words from the illustrated section of this book, along with their pronunciations and English translations.

Abbreviations such as **acc**, **dat**, **gen** and **pl** are used as throughout the book (see Key, page 3).

Nouns
Their plural endings are shown in brackets (see page 49 if you need to check how to form plurals using these brackets).

Verbs
* shows a verb that is irregular in the present tense; † shows a verb that is strong, mixed, or in some way irregular in the past tenses; separable verbs are shown with a/.

Pronunciation
The centre column shows you how to pronounce each word. The way to say the words properly is to imitate German speakers and apply the rules given on pages 4-5. However, by reading the

"words" in this column as if they were English, you will get a good idea of how to say things, or you will remember the sound of words you have heard before.

Note that, in this column, the German **ü** is shown as "ew". Remember, it is a little bit like the "u" in "music" (see page 4). The two different **ch** sounds (see page 5) are shown by "ch" (said like the "h" in "huge") and "kh" (said like the end of the Scottish word "loch").

A

abends	*ah-bends*	in the evening(s)
aber	*ah-ber*	but
ab/geben*†	*ab-gai-ben*	to hand in
abgeschlossen	*ab-ge-shloss-en*	locked
ab/hauen	*ab-how-en*	to clear off
ab/holen	*ab-hawl-en*	to fetch
die Adresse(n)	*dee adressa*	address
die Aktentasche(n)	*dee akten-tasha*	briefcase
alle	*alla*	all
allein	*a-lyne*	alone
allerseits	*aller-sytes*	(to) all of you, everyone
alles	*alass*	everything
als	*alss*	as (a), than, when
also	*al-zaw*	well then, right, so
alt	*alt*	old
am	*am*	(short for *an dem*)
Amerika	*a-mair-i-ka*	America
die Ampel(n)	*dee ampel*	set of traffic lights
sich amüsieren	*zich a-mew-zeer-en*	to enjoy yourself, to have fun/a good time
an	*an*	on, at
an/beten	*an-bai-ten*	to worship
der/die/das andere	*dair/dee/dass andara*	the other
an/fangen*†	*an-fang-en*	to start, to begin
an/kommen†	*an-komm-en*	to arrive
ans	*anz*	(short for *an das*)
an/schauen	*an-sh-ow-en*	to (go and) look at
sich (etwas) anschauen	*zich (etvass) an-sh-ow-en*	to (take a) look at (something)
an/sehen*†	*an-zai-en*	to look at
der Anteil(e)	*dair an-tyle*	share, portion
die Antwort(en)	*dee ant-vawrt*	answer
sich an/ziehen†	*zich an-tsee-en*	to get dressed
der Anzug(¨e)	*dair an-tsoog*	suit
der Apfel (¨)	*dair ap-fel*	apple
die Apotheke(n)	*dee a-paw-tai-ka*	chemist's shop, pharmacy
arbeiten	*ahr-by-ten*	to work
sich ärgern	*zich air-gern*	to be/get annoyed
der Artikel(-)	*dair ahr-tee-kel*	article
das Atelier(s)	*dass a-tel-ee-ai*	studio
auch	*owkh*	too, also
auf	*owf*	on, onto, on top of, in (for a language), up
auf diese Weise	*owf deeza vyza*	(in) this way
auf/essen*†	*owf-essen*	to eat up, to finish
die Aufgabe(n)	*dee owf-gah-ba*	task
auf/passen	*owf-passen*	to watch out, to pay attention
auf/räumen	*owf-roy-men*	to tidy up
aufs	*owfss*	(short for *auf das*)
auf/stehen†	*owf-shtai-en*	to get up
auf/wachen	*owf-vakhen*	to wake up
aus	*owss*	out of, from
der Ausflug(¨e)	*dair owss-floog*	outing, trip
der Ausgang(¨e)	*dair owss-gang*	exit
aus/geben*†	*owss-gai-ben*	to spend (money)
sich aus/ruhen	*zich owss-roo-en*	to have a rest, to relax
aus/sehen*†	*owss-zai-en*	to seem, to look

B

die Bäckerei(en)	*dee bekka-rye*	baker's shop
der Bahnhof(¨e)	*dair bahn-hawf*	station
bald	*balt*	soon
das Band(¨er)	*dass bant*	ribbon
die Bank(¨e)	*dee bank*	bench
bauen	*how-en*	to build
der Bauernhof(¨e)	*dair how-ern-hawf*	farm
der Baum(¨e)	*dair bowm*	tree
sich beeilen	*zich be-eylen*	to hurry
sich befinden†	*zich be-finden*	to be, to be found/ situated
begegnen [+ dat]	*be-gaig-nen*	to meet (bump into)
beginnen†	*be-ginnen*	to begin, to start
bei	*by*	near, at ...'s (someone's house)
beim	*bym*	(short for *bei dem*)
die beiden	*dee byden*	both (of them), the two
bekommen†	*be-kommen*	to receive, to get, to have babies/offspring
bellen	*bellen*	to bark
die Belohnung(en)	*dee be-lawn-ung*	reward
benutzen	*be-noo-tsen*	to use
der Berg(e)	*dair bairg*	mountain
sich beruhigen	*zich be-roo-i-gen*	to calm down
beschädigen	*be-shai-di-gen*	to damage
beschmutzen	*be-schmoo-tsen*	to dirty
besorgen	*be-zorg-en*	to get, to acquire
besser	*besser*	better
der/die/das beste	*dair/dee/dass besta*	the best
bestimmt	*be-shtimmt*	definitely
das Bett(en)	*dass bet*	bed
bevor	*be-fawr*	before
das Bild(er)	*dass bilt*	picture
bis	*biss*	until, as far as
bis bald	*biss balt*	see you soon
bis später	*biss shpai-ter*	see you later
bitte	*bitta*	please
Bitte schön?	*bitta shean*	What would you like?
bitten um†	*bitten um*	to ask for
blau	*bl-ow*	blue
bleiben†	*bly-ben*	to stay, to keep
bloß	*plawss*	merely, only
der Blumenkohl	*dair bloomen-kawl*	cauliflower
das Bonbon(s)	*dass bon(g)-bon(g)*	sweet, candy
das Boot(e)	*dass bawt*	boat
der Botaniker(-)	*dair bo-tah-ni-ker*	botanist
braun	*brown*	brown
brav	*brahv*	good, well behaved
der Brief(e)	*dair breef*	letter
die Brille(n)	*dee brilla*	(pair of) glasses
bringen†	*bringen*	to bring, to take
das Brot(e)	*dass brawt*	bread, loaf
das Brötchen(-)	*dass bru(r)-t-chen*	(bread) roll
die Brücke(n)	*dee brew-ka*	bridge
der Bruder(¨)	*dair broo-der*	brother
der Brunnen(-)	*dair broonnen*	fountain
das Buch(¨er)	*dass bookh*	book
der Buntstift(e)	*dair boont-shtift*	crayon

C

das Café(s)	*dass ka-fai*	café

der Campingplatz(¨e)	dair kemping-plats	campsite
die Cola	dee kaw-la	cola

D

da	dah	there
da drüben	dah drew-ben	there, over there
das Dach(¨er)	dass dakh	roof
dahin	dah-hin	(to) there
dahin/gehen†	dah-hin-gai-en	to go (to) there
(da)hinunter	(dah)-hin-oonter	down (there)
da/lassen*†	dah-lassen	to leave here/there
danke	danka	thank you
danke schön	danka-shu(r)n	thank you (very much)
dann	dann	then
das geht	dass gait	it's all right
das ist	dass isst	that is, it's
das macht nichts	dass makht nichts	it doesn't matter
das stimmt	dass shtimmt	that's right/true
dein, deine	dyne, dyna	your
denken†	deng-ken	to think
das Denkmal(¨er)	dass denk-mahl	monument
denn	denn	then
der, die, das, die	dair, dee, dass, dee	the
derselbe (dieselbe, dasselbe, dieselben)	dair-zelba (dee-zelba, dasselba, dee-zellben)	the (very) same
dich	dich	yourself
der Dieb(e)	dair deeb	thief
diese	deeza	these (ones)
diese da	deeza dah	those (ones)
dieser, diese, dieses	deezer, deeza, deeses	this, that, this/that one
doch	dokh	yet, but
der Dom(e)	dair dawm	cathedral
doof	dawf	stupid, silly
das Dorf(¨er)	dass dawrf	village
dort	dawrt	there
dort drüben	dawrt drew-ben	there, over there
draußen	drow-ssen	outside
dreckig	drekich	filthy, horrible
drehen	drai-en	to turn, to go around
drinnen	drinnen	inside
dritt- [+ ending]	dritt	third
du	doo	you
dumm	doomm	stupid
dummerweise	doomma-vyza	stupidly
dunkel	doonkel	dark
durch	doorch	through
durchfaxen	doorch-faxen	to fax through
dürfen*†	dewr-fen	to be allowed to, may

E

eben	ai-ben	just
echt	echt	genuine, real
eher	ai-er	sooner
die Eiche(n)	dee y-cha	oak (tree)
ein/eine	yne/yna	a
ein bißchen	yne biss-chen	a bit/little
ein paar	yne pahr	a few
der Einbrecher(-)	dair yne-brecher	burglar
einfach	yne-fahkh	simply, just
der Eingang(¨e)	dair yne-gang	entrance
ein/kaufen	yne-kowfen	to do some shopping
ein/kaufen gehen†	yne-kowfen gai-en	to go shopping
ein/schlagen*†	yne-shlah-gen	to break, to smash in
ein/stellen	yne-shtellen	to put away/in (the proper place)
einverstanden sein	ynfa-shtanden zyne	to agree
der Einwohner(-)	dair yne-vaw-ner	inhabitant
die Einzelheit(en)	dee yne-tsel-hyte	detail
das Eis	dass ice	ice cream
eisern	y-zern	iron
eiskalt	ice-kallt	ice-cold
die Eltern [pl]	dee ell-tern	parents
empfehlen*†	emp-fai-len	to recommend
das Ende	enn-da	end
enden	enn-den	to end
endlich	end-lich	at last
entlang	ent-lang	along, alongside
entlegen	ent-lai-gen	remote, isolated
entschuldige, entschuldigen Sie	ent-shooll-digga, ent-shooll-diggen zee	excuse me
Entschuldigung	ent-shooll-di-goong	excuse me, sorry
entziffern	ent-tsiff-ern	to decipher, to work out
er	air	he/it
die Erdbeere(n)	dee aird-bair-a	strawberry
die Erde	dee air-da	earth, soil, world
erforschen	air-fawr-shen	to explore
erhalten*†	air-hallten	to preserve, to maintain, to keep
erklären	air-klair-en	to explain
erreichen	air-rye-chen	to reach
erscheinen†	air-shy-nen	to appear, to seem
erst	airst	not until, only (for time or age)
der/die/das erste	dair/dee/dass air-sta	the first
erzählen	air-tsai-len	to tell, to talk
es geht ihnen gut	ess gait eenen goot	they're fine
es geht nicht	ess gait nicht	it's no good, it won't work
es gibt	ess gibt	there is/are
es ist	ess isst	it is, there is
essen*†	essen	to eat
das Essen	dass essen	food
etwas	et-vass	something
euer/eure	oyer/oyra	your

F

fahren*†	fah-ren	to go, to drive, to travel
das Fahrrad(¨er)	dass fahr-raht	bicycle
der Fahrschein(e)	dair fahr-shyne	ticket
fallen*†	fallen	to fall
fallen lassen†	fallen lass-en	to drop
falsch	fallsh	false, wrong
die Familie(n)	dee fa-mee-lee-a	family
fangen*†	fang-en	to catch
fassen	fass-en	to catch, to apprehend
fehlen	fai-len	to be missing
das Fenster(-)	dass fenn-ster	window
die Fensterscheibe(n)	dee fenn-ster-shy-ba	window-pane
die Ferien [pl]	dee fair-ee-en	holidays, vacations
das Fernglas(¨er)	dass fairn-glass	(pair of) binoculars
fertig	fair-tich	ready, finished
fest	fesst	tight, hard
die Festung(en)	dee fess-toong	fort, fortress
der Film(e)	dair film	film
finden†	finn-den	to find
fliegen†	flee-gen	to fly
der Flughafen(¨)	dair floog-hah-fen	airport
der Fluß (Flüsse)	dair flooss	river
folgen [+ dat]	folg-en	to follow
das Foto(s)	dass faw-taw	photo
der Fotoapparat(e)	dair faw-taw-appa-raht	camera
das Fotokopiergerät(e)	dass faw-taw-koppeer-ge-rait	photocopier
Fotos machen	faw-tawz makh-en	to take photos
die Frage(n)	dee frah-ga	question
fragen	frahg-en	to ask
die Frau(en)	dee frow	woman
Fräulein	froy-lyne	Miss
frei	fry	free
der Freund(e)	dair froynd	friend
die Freundin(nen) [f]	dee froyn-dinn	friend (girl)
das Frühstück(e)	dass frew-shtewk	breakfast
sich (wohl) fühlen	zich (vawl) few-len	to feel (well, happy)
für	fewr	for
der Fußball(¨e)	dair fooss-bal	football
der Fußgänger(-)	dair fooss-geng-er	pedestrian
der Fußgängerüberweg(e)	dair fooss-geng-er-ewber-vaig	pedestrian crossing

G

ganz	gants	entire, whole, all, quite, exactly
ganz allein	gants a-lyne	all alone
gar nicht	gahr nicht	not at all
der Garten(¨)	dair gahr-ten	garden
der Gauner(-)	dair gow-ner	crook, scoundrel

German	Pronunciation	English
das Gebäude(-)	dass ge-boy-da	building
geben*†	gai-ben	to give
gefährlich	ge-fair-lich	dangerous
gegen	gaig-en	against, towards
gegenüber	gaig-en-ew-ber	opposite
das Geheimnis(se)	dass ge-hyme-niss	secret
gehen†	gai-en	to go, to walk
gehören [+ dat]	ge-hu(r)-ren	to belong to
gelb	gelp	yellow
das Geld	dass gelt	money
der Geldschrank(¨e)	dair gelt-shrank	safe
gelingen†	ge-ling-en	to succeed
das Gemüse	dass ge-mew-za	vegetables
gemütlich	ge-mewt-lich	cosy, friendly, pleasant
genau	ge-now	exactly, exact
(genau)so ... wie	(ge-now)-zaw ... vee	(just) as ... as
genießen†	ge-nee-ssen	to enjoy
das Gepäck	dass ge-pek	luggage
gerade	ge-rah-da	just
geradeaus	ge-rah-da-owss	straight ahead, straight on
gern	gairn	gladly
das Geschäft(e)	dass ge-sheft	shop
geschehen*†	ge-shai-en	to happen
die Geschichte(n)	dee ge-shich-ta	story, history
geschlossen	ge-shloss-en	closed
das Gesicht(er)	dass ge-zicht	face
gestern	gess-tern	yesterday
gestern abend	gess-tern ah-bend	yesterday evening, last night
gestohlene Papiere	ge-shtaw-lenna pa-peer-a	stolen papers
das Gitter(-)	dass gitter	grid, bars
die Glatze(n)	dee gla-tsa	bald head/patch
gleich	glyche	right away, (the) same
Glück haben	glewk hah-ben	to be lucky
das Gold	dass gollt	gold
der Gouverneur(e)	dair goo-vair-nur	governor
gratulieren [+ dat]	gra-too-lee-ren	to congratulate (someone)
grau	gr-ow	grey
groß	graws	tall, big
großartig	grawss-ahr-tich	brilliant, terrific
die Großmutter(¨)	dee grawss-mootter	grandmother
der Großvater(¨)	dair grawss-fahter	grandfather
grün	grewn	green
gut	goot	good, well
guten Abend	goo-ten ah-bend	good evening
guten Tag	goo-ten tahg	hello

H

German	Pronunciation	English
haben*†	hah-ben	to have
der Hafen(¨)	dair hah-fen	port, harbour
halb eins	halp ynts	half past twelve
halb zwei	halp tsvy	half past one
hallo	ha-law	hello, hi
Halt!	hallt	stop!
die Hand(¨e)	dee hant	hand
das Handtuch(¨er)	dass hant-tookh	towel
der Handwerker(-)	dair hant-vair-ker	workman
das Haus(¨er)	dass howss	house
heißen†	hyssen	to be called
der Held(en)	dair hellt	hero
helfen*† [+ dat]	hell-fen	to help
das Hemd(en)	dass hemmt	shirt
herein/fallen*† auf [+ acc]	herryne fal-len owf	to fall for (something)
herein/tragen*†	herryne-trahg-en	to carry in
Herrn	hairrn	to Mr
herrschen	hairr-shen	to be (for weather)
heute	hoy-ta	today
heute abend	hoy-ta ah-bend	this evening, tonight
heute morgen	hoy-ta mawrg-en	this morning
hier	heer	here
hier spricht	heer shpricht	it's (here speaks)
hierher	heer-hair	(towards) here
hierüber	heer-ewber	over here
der Himmel	dair himmel	sky
hin und wieder	hin oont vee-der	now and again

German	Pronunciation	English
hinein/gehen†	hin-yne gai-en	to go, to come in
hinein/kommen†	hin-yne komm-en	to come, to get in
hinter	hin-ter	behind
hinterlassen*†	hin-ter-lass-en	to leave behind
hinunter/gehen†	hin-oonter-gai-en	to go down
der Hinweis(e)	dair hin-vyze	clue, tip
(höchst)wahrscheinlich	(hea-chst)-vahr-shyne-lich	(most) probably
hoffentlich	hoff-ent-lich	I/we hope, with hope
die Höhle(n)	dee hu(r)-la	cave
holen	haw-len	to fetch
die Hose(n)	dee haw-za	(pair of) trousers
die Hosentasche(n)	dee haw-zen-ta-sha	trouser pocket
das Hotel(s)	dass haw-tell	hotel
hübsch	hewpsh	pretty
der Hügel(-)	dair hew-g(u)l	hill
der Hund(e)	dair hoont	dog
der Hüpfer(-)	dair hewp-fer	hop, skip

I

German	Pronunciation	English
ich	ich	I
ideal	ee-dai-ahl	perfect, ideal
die Idee(n)	dee ee-dai	idea
im	im	(short for in dem)
im Kreis	im kryze	in a circle, in circles
im Schatten	im shatten	in the shade
immer	immer	always
in	in	in, into
in der Nähe von	in dair nai-a fonn	near
in Ordnung	in awrd-nung	fine, OK
der Inhaber(-)	dair in-hah-ber	proprietor, owner
innen drin	innen drinn	inside
ins	innz	(short for in das)
die Insel(n)	dee inn-zel	island
die Inselgruppe(n)	dee inn-zel-grooppa	group of islands, archipelago
interessant	interess-ant	interesting, exciting
irgendwo	eerg-endvaw	somewhere
ist	isst	is

J

German	Pronunciation	English
ja	yyah	yes
die Jacke(n)	dee yya-ka	jacket
das Jahr(e)	dass yyahr	year
... Jahre alt	... yyah-ra allt	... years old
die Jeans [pl]	dee jeens	jeans
jedenfalls	yyai-den-falz	anyhow
jetzt	yyetst	now
jung	yyoong	young
das Juwel(en)	dass yyoo-vail	jewel

K

German	Pronunciation	English
der Kaffee	dair kaff-ai	coffee
der Kai(e or s)	dair kye	quay
das Kalb(¨er)	dass kalp	calf
der Kampf(¨e)	dair kampf	battle
kaputt	kaput	broken
die Karte(n)	dee kahr-ta	map, card, ticket
der Karton(s)	dair kahr-ton(g)	cardboard box
der Käse	dair kai-za	cheese
der Kassettenrecorder(-)	dair kass-ett-en-re-kawr-der	cassette recorder
die Katze(n)	dee ka-tsa	cat
kaufen	kowfen	to buy
kein, keine	kyne, kyna	not a, not any, no
Keine Sorge!	kyna zawr-ga	Don't worry!
kennen†	kennen	to know
der Kerker(-)	dair kair-ker	dungeon
die Kerze(n)	dee kair-tsa	candle
das Kilo	dass kee-law	kilo
das Kind(er)	dass kinnt	child, kid
das Kino(s)	dass kee-naw	cinema
die Kirche(n)	dee kair-cha	church
die Kiste(n)	dee kiss-ta	chest, case, crate
klar	klah(r)	clear

Klasse!	*klassa*	great!
das Kleid(er)	*dass klyde*	dress
die Kleider [pl]	*dee kly-der*	clothes
klein	*klyne*	short, small
die Klementine(n)	*dee klem-en-tee-na*	clementine
klettern	*klettern*	to climb, to clamber
der Koffer(-)	*dair koffer*	suitcase
der Kollege(n)	*dair koll-aiga*	colleague, fellow-
komisch	*kaw-mish*	funny, strange, odd
kommen†	*kommen*	to come
können*†	*ku(r)-nen*	to be able to, can
die Kopfschmerztablette(n)	*kopf-shmairts-tab-letta*	aspirin, headache pill
der Korb(¨e)	*dair kawrb'*	basket
kosten	*koss-ten*	to cost
kräftig	*kreff-tich*	strong, powerful
krank	*krank*	ill
der Kratzer(-)	*dair kratser*	scratch
der Krebs(e)	*dair kraibs*	crab
die Kreuzung(en)	*dee kroy-tsung*	crossroads, junction
der Kuchen(-)	*dair koo-khen*	cake
die Kuh(¨e)	*dee koo*	cow
der Kumpel(-)	*dair koomm-pel*	mate, good friend
der Kurier(e)	*dair koo-reer*	messenger
kurz	*koorts*	short
die Küste(n)	*dee kew-sta*	coast

L

lachen	*la-khen*	to laugh
das Land(¨er)	*dass lant*	country, land
die Landkarte(n)	*dee lant-kahrta*	map
die Landschaft [no pl]	*dee lant-shafft*	landscape
lang	*lang*	long
langsam	*lang-zam*	slowly
das Laub [no pl]	*dass l-ow-b*	leaves, foliage
laufen*†	*lowf-en*	to run, to walk
laut	*lout*	loud(ly)
leb wohl	*laib vawl*	farewell
leer	*lair*	empty
legen	*laig-en*	to put (lay down)
der Lehrer(-)	*dair lairer*	teacher
leicht	*lychte*	easy
leichter Diebstahl [m]	*lychter deeb-shtahl*	petty theft
leider	*lyder*	unfortunately
leihen†	*ly-en*	to hire, to lend
sich (etwas) leihen†	*zich (et-vass) ly-en*	to borrow (something)
lesen*†	*lai-zen*	to read
der/die/das letzte	*dair/dee/dass let-sta*	the last
die Leute [pl]	*dee loyta*	people
das Licht(er)	*dass licht*	light
lieb	*leeb*	dear
Leiber [+ m name], **Liebe** [+ f name]	*leeber, leeba*	Dear ...
lieber	*leeber*	more gladly, preferably
Liebling	*leeb-ling*	darling, dear
Lieblings-	*leeb-lings*	favourite (adds on to front of noun)
die Limonade	*dee lee-maw-nah-da*	lemonade
links	*links*	(on the) left
der Lohn(¨e)	*dair lawn*	wage, fee
die Luft	*dee loofft*	air
die Lupe(n)	*dee loo-pa*	magnifying glass

M

machen	*makhen*	to do, to make
man	*man*	one, you
der Mann(¨er)	*dair man*	man
die Mansarde(n)	*dee man-ssahr-da*	attic
die Mark(-)	*dee mahrk*	mark (German money)
der Markt(¨e)	*dair mahrkt*	market
die Mauer(n)	*dee m-ow-er*	wall (outside wall)
der Mechaniker(-)	*dair me-chah-niker*	mechanic
das Meer(e)	*dass mair*	sea
mehr	*mair*	more
der/die/das meiste	*dair/dee/dass mysta*	(the) most
Mensch!	*mensh*	Hey!, Wow!, Man!
mich	*mich*	myself, me

mit	*mit*	with
mit Holzplatten verkleidet	*mit hollts-platten fer-kly-det*	with wooden panels
(zusammen) mit	*(tsoo-zammen) mit*	(together) with
mit/bringen†	*mit-bringen*	to bring along/with
mit/kommen†	*mit-kommen*	to come along/with
Mittag	*mittahg*	midday, noon
das Mittagessen(-)	*dass mittahg-essen*	lunch
Mitternacht	*mitter-nahkht*	midnight
mögen*†	*mu(r)g-en*	to like
der Monat(e)	*dair maw-naht*	month
morgen	*mawrgen*	tomorrow
morgen früh	*mawrgen frew*	tomorrow morning
morgens	*mawrgens*	in the morning(s)
müde	*mewda*	tired
der Müller(-)	*dair mewller*	miller
müssen*†	*mewssen*	to have to, must
die Mutter(¨)	*dee mootter*	mother
Mutti	*moottee*	Mum(my)
die Mütze(n)	*dee mewtsa*	cap

N

na	*na*	now then, well
na gut	*na goot*	right, well, OK
nach	*nahkh*	after, to (used with a place name)
nach Hause	*nahkh how-za*	home
nach links/rechts	*nahkh links/rechts*	(to the) left/right
der Nachbar(n)	*dair nahkh-bahr*	neighbour
nach/denken†	*nahkh-deng-ken*	to think, to ponder
nachmittags	*nahkh-mi-tahgs*	in the afternoon(s)
nach/sehen*†	*nahkh-zai-en*	to have a look
der/die/das nächste	*dair/dee/dass nech-sta*	the nearest/next
die Nacht(¨e)	*dee nahkht*	night
die Nagelfeile(n)	*dee nahgel-fyla*	nail file
nah	*nah*	near
die Nähe [no pl]	*dee nai-a*	vicinity
näher	*nai-er*	nearer
namens	*nah-mens*	called
naß	*nass*	wet
natürlich	*na-tewr-lich*	of course, naturally
neben	*nai-ben*	next to, adjacent
nehmen*†	*nai-men*	to take
nein	*nyne*	no
nett	*net*	nice, kind
das Netz(e)	*dass nets*	net
neu	*noy*	new
nicht	*nicht*	not
nicht mehr	*nicht mair*	not any more, no longer
nichts	*nichts*	nothing
nie(mals)	*nee(mahlz)*	never
niemand	*nee-mand*	nobody, no one
noch	*nokh*	still
noch nicht	*nokh nicht*	not yet
normalerweise	*nawr-mah-ler-vyza*	normally
die Nummer(n)	*dee noommer*	number
nun	*noon*	now
nur	*noor*	only

O

ohne	*aw-na*	without
das Ohr(en)	*dass awr*	ear
oje!	*aw-yyai*	oh dear!, oh no!
die Orange(n)	*dee oronja*	orange
der Orangensaft	*dair oronjen-zaft*	orange juice

P

das Paar(e)	*dass pahr*	pair
der Papagei(en)	*dair pa-pa-guy*	parrot
das Papier(e)	*dass pa-peer*	paper
der Park(s)	*dair pahrk*	park
passieren	*passeer-en*	to happen
(So ein) Pech!	*(zaw yne) pech*	(What) bad luck!
perfekt	*pair-fekt*	perfect

German	Pronunciation	English
die Pflanze(n)	dee pflantsa	plant
das Pflaster(-)	dass pflasster	plaster
der Pirat(en)	dair pee-raht	pirate
der Platz(¨e)	dair platts	square
die Polizei	dee pol-lits-eye	police
der (Polizei)- kommissar(e)	dair (pol-lits-eye)- kom-miss-ahr	(police) inspector
die Polizeiwache(n)	dee pol-lits-eye-vahkha	police station
Pommes frites [pl]	pomm fritt	chips, French fries
das Porträt(s)	dass pawr-trai	portrait
die Postkarte(n)	dee posst-kahr-ta	postcard
probieren	pro-bee-ren	to try, to have a taste
die Prüfung(en)	dee prew-foong	exam(ination)
der Pulli(s)	dair pull-ee	jumper
der Pullover(-)	dair pull-awver	jumper

R

German	Pronunciation	English
die Rache	dee rakha	revenge
rar	rahr	rare, scarce
sich rasieren	zich ra-zee-ren	to shave
rauchen	row-khen	to smoke
rechts	rechts	(on the) right
regnen	raig-nen	to rain
reich	ryche	rich, wealthy
reichen	rychen	to be enough, to reach, to pass
der Reiseführer(-)	dair ryzer-fewrer	guidebook
reparieren	rai-pa-ree-ren	to repair, to mend
reparieren lassen	rai-pa-ree-ren lassen	to have/get ... repaired
das Restaurant(s)	dass rest-aw-ro	restaurant
richtig	rich-tich	right, correct
die Richtung(en)	dee rich-toong	direction
der Riemen(-)	dair ree-men	oar
der Ring(e)	dair ring	ring
rostig	rostich	rusty
rot	rawt	red
der Rucksack(¨)	dair rook-zak	rucksack
rudern	roo-dern	to row
ruhig	roo-ich	calm, quiet
die Ruine(n)	dee roo-eena	ruin

S

German	Pronunciation	English
sagen	zahgen	to say
die Salbe(n)	dee zalba	ointment
die Sammlung(en)	dee zamm-loong	collection
schaffen	shaffen	to manage
der Schatz(¨e)	dair shats	treasure
Schätzchen	shets-chen	darling, dear
die Schatzsuche	dee shats-zoo-kha	treasure hunt
schau, schau mal	sh-ow, sh-ow mahl	look
schauen	sh-owen	to look
scheinen†	shy-nen	to shine, to seem
schicken	shikken	to send
das Schiff(e)	dass shiff	ship
das Schloß (Schlösser)	dass shloss (shlu(r)sser)	castle, lock
der Schlüssel(-)	dair shlewssel	key
schnappen	shnappen	to catch, to nab
(durch)/schneiden†	(doorch)-shny-den	to cut (through)
schnell	shnell	quick(ly), fast
der/das Schnitzel(-)	dair/dass shnitsel	bit, scrap
schon	shawn	already
schon gut	shawn goot	all right, OK
schön	shean	right, well, OK, lovely, beautiful
schöne Ferien	shu(r)na fair-ee-en	(have a) nice holiday
der Schuh(e)	dair shoo	shoe
die Schule(n)	dee shoola	school
die Schüssel(n)	dee shewssel	bowl
schwarz	shvahrts	black
die Schwester(n)	dee shvester	sister
schwierig	shvee-rich	difficult
das Schwimmbad(¨er)	dass shvimm-bahd	swimming pool
schwimmen†	shvimmen	to swim
der See(n)	dair zai	lake
sehen*†	zai-en	to see, to look at
sehr	zair	very (much), a lot
Sehr geehrte(r) ...	zair ge-air-ta	Dear ... (formal)
das Seil(e)	dass zyle	rope

German	Pronunciation	English
sein*†	zyne	to be
seit	zyte	since
selten	zellten	rare(ly), seldom
setzen	zetsen	to put (set down)
sich setzen	zich zetsen	to sit (yourself) down
die Shorts [pl]	dee shorrts	shorts
Sie	zee	you
sie	zee	she/it/they
sind	zint	are
singen†	zingen	to sing
die Sitzung(en)	dee zitsoong	meeting
so	zaw	like this/that, so
sofort	zawfort	straight away
der Sohn(¨e)	dair zawn	son
sollen*	zollen	should, to be supposed to
die Sonne	dee zonna	sun
die Spalte(n)	dee shpalta	crack
spannend	shpannend	exciting
spät	shpait	late
später	shpaiter	later
der Speck	dair shpek	(bacon) fat, flab
die Speisekarte(n)	dee spyza-kahr-ta	menu
spielen	shpee-len	to play
die Spielkarte(n)	dee shpeel-kahr-ta	(playing) card
sprechen*†	shprechen	to speak, to talk
die Spur(en)	dee shpoor	trail, track
die Stadt(¨e)	dee shtat	town
stehen†	shtai-en	to stand, to be (standing)
stehlen*†	shtailen	to steal
steigen†	shty-g-en	to climb, to go up
der Steine(e)	dair shtyne	stone, rock
sterben*†	shtairben	to die
stören	shtu(r)ren	to disturb, to get in the way
stoßen*† [auf + acc]	shtawssen (owf)	to find (by chance), to come across
der Strand(¨e)	dair shtrand	beach
die Straße(n)	dee shtrahssa	road, street
die Sturmzeit(en)	dee shtoorm-tsyte	stormy season
stürzen	shtewr-tsen	to fall, to plunge
suchen	zookhen	to look for
der Supermarkt(¨e)	dair zooper-mahrkt	supermarket
die Suppe(n)	dee zooppa	soup
das Sweatshirt(s)	dass svet-sheart	sweatshirt

T

German	Pronunciation	English
die Tablette(n)	dee ta-bletta	tablet, aspirin
der Tag(e)	dair tahg	day
das Tagebuch(¨er)	dass tah-ge-bookh	diary
der Tagesablauf	dair tahg-ess-ab-l-ow-f	events of the day
die Tante(n)	dee tanta	aunt
tanzen	tantsen	to dance
die Tasche(n)	dee tasha	bag, pocket
die Taschenlampe(n)	dee tashen-lampa	torch, flashlight
der Tee	dair tai	(cup of) tea
das Teil(e)	dass tyle	spare part
der Tempel(-)	dair tempel	temple
teuer	toy-er	expensive
der Tisch(e)	dair tish	table
toll	toll	great
das Tor(e)	dass tawr	gate
die Torte(n)	dee tawrta	gateau, cake
tot	tawt	dead
tragen*†	trahgen	to carry, to wear
der Trainingsanzug(¨e)	dair trai-nings-an-zoog	tracksuit
die Trainingsschuhe [pl]	dee trai-nings-shoo-a	trainers
treffen*†	treffen	to meet
die Treppe(n)	dee treppa	(flight of) steps
trinken†	tring-ken	to drink
das T-shirt(s)	dass tee-shu(r)rt	T-shirt
das Tuch(¨er)	dass tookh	towel, cloth
tun*†	toon	to do
der Tunnel(-)	dair toonnel	tunnel
die Tür(en)	dee tewr	door
der Turm(¨e)	dair toorm	tower
der Typ	dair tewp	bloke, guy

U

über	ewber	over, across
überall	ewber-al	everywhere
die Überfahrt(en)	dee ewber-fahrt	(sea) crossing
überhaupt	ewber-howpt	anyhow, at all
... Uhr	oor	... o'clock
die Uhr(en)	dee oor	clock
um	oom	around, at
Um wieviel Uhr?	oom veefeel oor	(At) what time?
um ... zu	oom ... tsoo	to, in order to
umsonst	oom-zonst	(for) free
und	oont	and
(un)glücklicherweise	(oon)glewk-licher-vyza	(un)luckily, (un)fortunately
unter	oonter	under (among)
der Untermieter(-)	dair oonter-mee-ter	lodger
untersuchen	oonter-zoo-khen	to examine
der Urgroßvater(¨)	dair oor-grawss-fah-ter	great-grandfather

V

der Vater(¨)	dair fahter	father
Vati	fah-tee	Dad(dy)
der Verbrecher(-)	dair fair-brecher	criminal
verbringen†	fair-bringen	to spend (time)
verdecken	fair-dekken	to cover, to hide
vergessen*†	fair-gessen	to forget
verhaftet sein	fair-haf-tet zyne	to be under arrest
verlassen	fair-lassen	deserted, desert
verlieren†	fair-leeren	to lose
das Vermögen(-)	dass fair-mu(r)gen	fortune
verpacken	fair-pakken	to wrap (up)
verschwinden†	fair-shvinden	to disappear
das Verschwinden	dass fair-shvinden	disappearance
das Versteck(e)	dass fair-shtek	hiding-place
verstecken	fair-shtekken	to hide
sich verstecken	zich fair-shtekken	to hide (yourself)
versteckt	fair-shtekkt	hidden
verstehen†	fair-shtai-en	to understand, to see
vertreiben†	fair-try-ben	to expel, to drive out
viel	feel	much, many, a lot, lots of
viele Grüße	feela grewssa	best wishes, love from
vielen Dank	feelen dank	many thanks
vielleicht	fee-lychte	perhaps, maybe
Viertel vor/nach eins	feer-tel fawr/nahkh yntse	(a) quarter to/past one
der Vogel(¨)	dair fawg-el	bird
vom	fomm	(short for von dem)
von	fonn	from, of, by
vor	fawr	in front of, before
vor [+ dat]	fawr	ago
vorher	fawr-hair	before(hand)
vormittags	fawrmi-tahgs	in the morning(s)
vor/schieben†	fawr-sheeben	to push (...) in front

W

wachsen*†	vaxen	to grow
während [+ gen]	vair-end	during
wahrscheinlich	vahr-shyne-lich	probably
der Wald(¨er)	dair vald	forest
die Wand(¨e)	dee vand	wall
wann	vann	when
warten	vahr-ten	to wait
warum	vahr-roomm	why
was	vass	what
was für?	vass fewr	what kind/sort of?
Was ist das?	vass isst dass	What is that?
sich waschen*†	zich vashen	to have a wash

der Weg(e)	dair vaig	path, way, lane
wegen [+ gen or dat]	vaig-en	because of
die Weihnachtsferien [pl]	dee vy-nakhts-fair-ee-en	Christmas holidays
weil	vyle	because
weiß	vysse	white
weiter	vyter	further
weiter/machen	vyter-makhen	to carry on, continue
welcher	vellcher	which
Wem gehört/ gehören ...?	vaim ge-hu(r)rt/ge-hu(r)ren	Who does/do [...] belong to?, Whose is/are ...?
wenn	venn	if, when, whenever
wer	vair	who
werden*†	vairden	to become
werfen*†	vairfen	to throw
das Werkzeug(e)	dass vairk-tsoyg	tool
wessen	vessen	whose
wie	vee	how
Wie spät ist es?	vee shpait isst ess	what time is it?
(auf) Wiederhören	(owf) veeder-hu(r)ren	goodbye (on phone)
(auf) Wiedersehen	(owf) veeder-zai-en	goodbye
wieviel	vee-feel	how much
Wieviel Uhr ist es?	vee-feel oor isst ess	What time is it?, What's the time?
wieviele	vee-feela	how many
wir	veer	we
wirklich	veerk-lich	really, real
wissen*†	vissen	to know
der Witz(e)	dair vits	joke
wo	vaw	where, whereabouts
woher	vaw-hair	where from, how
wohnen	vaw-nen	to live
wollen*	vollen	to want
der Würfel(-)	dair vewr-fel	die (pl dice)

Z

zahlen	tsah-len	to pay
der Zauberer(-)	dair tsow-berer	magician
der Zaun(¨e)	dair tsown	fence
zehn	tsain	ten
das Zeichen(-)	dass tsychen	sign
zeigen	tsyg-en	to show
die Zeit(en)	dee tsyte	time
die Zeitung(en)	dee tsy-toong	newspaper
das Zelt(e)	dass tsellt	tent
zerreißen†	tsair-ryssen	to tear up
zerrissen	tsair-rissen	torn up
zerstören	tsair-shtu(r)ren	to destroy
zerstört	tsair-shtu(r)rt	destroyed, ruined
der Zettel(-)	dair tsettel	note, piece of paper
die Ziege(n)	dee tseega	goat
ziehen† [an + dat]	tsee-en	to pull, to give ... a pull
ziemlich	tseem-lich	fairly, quite
das Zimmer(-)	dass tsimmer	room
zu	tsoo	too, closed
zu	tsoo	to, to X's (someone's house)
[dat +] zu Ehren	tsoo airen	in ...'s honour
zu Hause	tsoo how-za	at home
zuerst	tsoo-airst	first of all, at first
zufällig	tsoo-fellich	by chance
der Zug(¨e)	dair tsoog	train
zu/machen	tsoo-makhen	to close, to shut
zur Zeit	tsoor tsyte	at the time, at the moment
zurück/gehen†	tsoo-rewk-gai-en	to go back
zurück/kommen†	tsoo-rewk-komm-en	to come back
der/die/das zweite	dair/dee/dass tsvyta	the second
zwischen	tsvishen	between
der Zylinder(-)	dair tsew-linder	top hat

First published in 1992 by Usborne Publishing Ltd.
Usborne House, 83–85 Saffron Hill, London EC1N 8RT, England
Copyright © 1992 Usborne Publishing Ltd.

Printed in Great Britain.